The next big thing

Judy Waite grew up in England and in Singapore. She studied graphic art at college, but after teaching graphics at a summer camp she discovered she loved working with children, and changed careers. Her love of writing stems from childhood, although she only began writing professionally in 1997. She writes for children of all ages, and has now had over thirty titles published. Her fiction has won several awards, including the English Association Best Picture Book Award in 1998 and The Nevada Young Readers' Award in 2001. Judy also works part-time in a junior school, and teaches creative writing at university. She has two teenage daughters. *The Next Big Thing* is her fourth novel for Oxford Univerisity Press.

Other books by Judy Waite

Shopaholic
A Trick of the Mind
Forbidden

The next big thing

Judy Waite

OXFORD
UNIVERSITY PRESS

Great Clarendon Street, Oxford OX2 6DP

Oxford University Press is a department of the University of Oxford.
It furthers the University's objective of excellence in research, scholarship,
and education by publishing worldwide in

Oxford New York

Auckland Cape Town Dar es Salaam Hong Kong Karachi
Kuala Lumpur Madrid Melbourne Mexico City Nairobi
New Delhi Shanghai Taipei Toronto

With offices in
Argentina Austria Brazil Chile Czech Republic France Greece
Guatemala Hungary Italy Japan Poland Portugal Singapore
South Korea Switzerland Thailand Turkey Ukraine Vietnam

Oxford is a registered trade mark of Oxford University Press
in the UK and in certain other countries

First published 2005

British Library Cataloguing in Publication Data

Data available

ISBN-13: 978-0-19-275393-2
ISBN-10: 0-19-275393-2

1 3 5 7 9 10 8 6 4 2

Typeset in Meridien by
Palimpsest Book Production Limited,
Polmont, Stirlingshire
Printed by Cox and Wyman Ltd, Reading, Berkshire

For Jason

I would like to thank the following people who generously gave both their time and expertise to help with research for this book:

Matt Green, Artist Management, London;

Geoff Webb, The Dug-out Studios, Fort Fareham, Hampshire;

Paul Nelson, The Wedgwood Rooms, Albert Road, Southsea, Hampshire;

Hayley Trent, *Top of the Pops*, BBC Television Studios, Wood Lane, London.

WANTED

LONDON BASED PRODUCTION
COMPANY SEEKS

Vocalists/
Guitarists

Male and Female

AGE BETWEEN 16 & 22

AUDITIONS TO BE HELD
SUNDAY 24TH
OCTOBER

The Circle Hotel, Crossford Lane, Newton

10a.m. — 5p.m.

Chapter One

The door opens.

A guy wearing a 'Pineapple Promotions' badge on his crisp cream jacket leans out: 'Number ninety-six.'

Elliot Heath watches the girl next to him stand up and hump her guitar over her shoulder. The promotions guy runs his hand backwards through his streaked blond hair, flicks a brief look at the girl, then leads her away into the audition suite.

Elliot's gut is knotted and his hands are shaking. He's next, and he isn't ready. His voice will lock. His strings will break. He'll mess up on the lyrics.

All around him performers are tuning up. Singing softly. Some not so soft. A guy with dreadlocks closes his eyes and hums, a dark drone of sound that runs on and on. There is a crush over near the mirror.

Standing, Elliot paces the length of the faded blue carpet, nearly colliding with Dreadlocks.

'Sorry, mate.'

'Sorry.'

They shake hands and Elliot thinks about soldiers in wars. Opposite sides of the wire. He doesn't like this mood. Doesn't want it. But he understands it.

He wonders now if he should have thought more

about his clothes. Sorted his hair out. He might sound the part, but does he look it? What do they want? How should he be? Number 96 is taking for ever. Elliot swallows and his throat is full of sand. His song will sound all scratched and sore.

Water. He needs water. There are jugs lined up on a table by the front desk, next to the 'personal details' forms that an anorexic-looking receptionist was handing out earlier. He heads for them, passing behind a girl in a denim cap, a spill of gold hair corkscrewing down over a green velvet jacket daubed with wild roses. 'Sorry,' he nods at her, catching the awkward lope of his stride in the mirror opposite. He's too tall. Too dark. Is it bad luck to cross paths in glass?

He is still shaking. The jugged water spills, knocking the plastic cup, and the 'personal details' forms get soggy and stained. He shoots out a panicked look, trying to catch the eye of the anorexic receptionist, but she is talking to a bloke in the corner, fussing with his hair.

'Don't worry. It's OK. I'll help.' He turns to see the wild roses girl standing beside him. She has amazing eyes. Turquoise eyes. Like pieces of the sky.

'I'll mop it.' She dabs at the forms with her sleeve, and her smile as she glances up at him is warm honey. 'I'm wobbling too. The idea of singing to a panel of strangers . . .'

Elliot doesn't want to make conversation. He should be saving his voice. And anyway, he's done with girls. Since Amber. Fox-red hair and moon-pale skin, Amber was bad news. All girls are bad news. But this one is still smiling, looking for some sort of a response. He has to give her something. 'This is my first audition.'

'Mine too.' She tilts her head at him. 'What are you singing?'

'A Marc Wild number. "Too Late". Off his last album—"Lost and Still Looking".' He thinks she'll know it—can't believe anyone would have got this far through life without knowing it—but she shakes her head.

'I haven't heard that before.'

'I like it. It's gut-wrenching, I guess.' As he says it the thought whips through him that gut-wrenching might be a bad choice. Maybe the production company wants skippy hoppy. Light and loveable.

'Mine's just easy.' Her reasoning confirms his skippy hoppy fear. 'I'm not good enough to take risks.'

Elliot is panicking again, thinking he's not good enough for risks either, but someone pokes him in the back. 'You number ninety-seven?' A cropped-haired guy with tattoos eyes the numbered sticker on Elliot's sleeve. 'They've called you twice.'

'Oh—right. OK.' Elliot swings round to where the promotions guy is standing over by the door again.

'Good luck.' Wild Roses touches his arm.

'Thanks.' He shoulders his guitar and pushes his way through. This is the moment. This is the chance.

'I'm Kris Kowper.' The promotions guy has dark wire eyebrows and glint-green eyes and he leads Elliot into the room where three people sit waiting behind a long wooden table. 'This'll be the production team once—or if—we make a decision. We've got together for the project. Normally we all work independently.'

A woman in chandelier earrings stands up and shakes his hand. 'Hi. I'm Wendy Sims. Did you fill in your form?' Her red lipstick mouth stretches a smile. 'Sophie—the girl on the desk—should have given you one when you came in.'

'I . . . yeah.' He fumbles in his jacket pocket. 'Here.'

He notices the stack of forms already piled up in front of her.

The chandelier earrings shiver as she skims the bones of his life. She looks up. 'Studying contemporary music. And you've been in a band. Have you always been musical?'

'Sort of. I get it from my dad. He sings.' The last bit is desperate. A grasp at any handhold. If they knew about Dad, would it make any difference? Would it make it worse? 'I can do anything. I write my own stuff and . . .'

'We don't need original material.' The guy next to Chandeliers has rheumy eyes, as if he's lived his life in smoke-choked rooms.

Chandeliers laces her fingers across the tabletop, a tiny fence between her and Elliot. He is thinking he is not coming over well. 'We're looking for a particular sound, and a particular look . . .' She glances across at Kris Kowper.

Elliot glances at him too. He is leaning back in his chair, his hands behind his head. Just watching.

'. . . We need someone to fit in with a team,' Chandeliers finishes.

'Yeah. That's fine.' Elliot nods to show her this *is* fine. He can do teams. He can fit in.

The fourth panellist leans forward suddenly, his face peering out through a bush of ginger beard. 'Stand over there. Just behind you. On the white cross.'

Elliot backs up to where two strips of tape are marking the spot on the floor. There are video screens either side of him and he catches that awkward lope again as he moves. He's feeling sick.

'When you're ready. Just one verse is all we need.' Ginger beard nods at him.

'It's a Marc Wild song.' Elliot fumbles with the case of his guitar. 'Called "Too Late".'

Chandeliers nods. None of them speak.

He plays the first chord but his voice is glued to the back of his throat. They are getting the scrapings of it. Sticky and thin. 'Sorry.' He jerks his head as if the action can jolt his voice free. 'I'll have another go.' He manages, just about, not to say 'please'. He's not begging yet.

'Just take your time.' Chandeliers smiles.

Kris Kowper glances at his watch.

Elliot makes another start, coming in too fast. Racing himself. His voice comes through stronger, but he still knows he's blown it. 'Too Late' should be slow. Edged with pain. The end of something beautiful. He's given it as much depth as 'Three Blind Mice'. 'Sorry—I'll go again.'

'No thanks. That's great. I reckon we've got what

we need.' Kris Kowper stands, already moving for the door.

Please. Please.

Chandeliers is patting his form down on to the top of the pile. Ninety-seven forms, and at least another twenty out there, waiting to be added. She smiles a goodbye at Elliot, but her eyes won't meet his.

Elliot glances across at the other two. Neither of them look up.

'Next please. Number ninety-eight.' Kris Kowper stands back to let Elliot pass.

Across the room the wild roses girl is laughing up at Dreadlocks. No point intruding. No point saying goodbye.

He shifts his guitar higher on to his shoulder, walking out through the glass swing doors and into the October afternoon. The sky is fierce blue and blustering, leaves and old litter stuttering along the road.

Words blow through his head, shaping into a tune. Fumbling for his notebook, he tries to scribble the lines. Then he scrubs them, scrunching at the page and spinning it down into the gutter. Let the cars roll over it. Flatten it. It is only more rubbish. He's suddenly sure he'd have been OK if they'd let him have another go. *Please*. *Please*. Too late. Too frigging late.

Just a number,
nameless face.
Words I'd woven
gone to waste.

Chapter Two

Paige Melder watches the tall, dark-haired boy swing out of the audition room, shoot a quick, pained glance round at the straggle of waiting kids, then walk away. She can see from his face that it hasn't gone well and she half wants to follow him—there're great stories in failure—but his mood looks so set and dark that she shrugs and decides against it. He'd be hard work and there isn't any point wearing herself out on this assignment. Especially as last night's party is still throbbing through her head. Boring Brian will edit out half of what she writes anyway—he wouldn't know a decent story from a page in the dictionary. How the hell did he ever make it to editor?

And it's a rubbish deal to have been sent out here on a Sunday. Why couldn't they have sent Yakini Knight? She's got all that new girl 'bounce and bubble'. She's only come in as an office junior but she's into music in a big way. She'd probably think it was great.

Paige scratches the edge of one fingernail with her thumb, annoyed that last night's varnish is already flaking off. Is this job really what she slogged away at Uni for? If she'd known that, two whole years later, she'd be stuck working for a pathetic local paper with a brain-dead boss and a team of reporters who thought the highlight of the week was to cover the local lollipop lady's retirement do, she might not have spent all that time slaving for her media studies degree. It feels like such a waste now.

She turns her attention back to a girl in a velvet flowered jacket talking to a boy with dreadlocks. The girl looks arty and will probably be too intense, but the boy might be worth a line or two. She could go for the ethnic angle. Although on second thoughts 'ethnic' won't sell papers in Newton. The locals are far too stuffy and middle class. In the end she picks on a girl in a gold spangled top who's watching herself sing in the mirror.

'Hi—I'm Paige Melder, *Newton News*.' She hands across a card. 'I just wondered if I could ask you a few questions?'

The girl wavers on her final note, glances at the card, and flicks out the self-conscious smile of someone who thinks they might be about to be photographed. 'Sure,' she nods, then giggles. 'Although don't write it down if I say anything stupid.'

Paige smiles back, pen poised. The stupider the better. 'Of course not.'

'I'm pretty nervous.' The girl is gabbling. 'It's nearly my turn and I'm sure . . .'

Paige Melder lets her run on about auditions she's done. How she's sung in bars. How it's so hard to break through to the next level. She jots down a spidered scrawl of notes, but she's hardly listening. She's got to get off this paper. She's got to get herself up to London. That's where she should be—sniffing out stories from underneath bricks and old stones and then laying them out in the burn of the sun. That's what she should be doing. She wouldn't mind working weekends for that.

Chapter Three

Elliot's mood clouds round him. He walks quickly and he doesn't look up. Doesn't see the gang. Not until it's too late to dodge or cross the road.

'You from here?' The leader kicks at the soft mush of leaves that clogs the mouth of the alley. Four followers in hoods and torn denims pad up behind him.

Elliot stops and faces the gang. The leader has pale eyes. Wolf's eyes. Elliot thinks they would glow in the dark. 'No.'

'Where then?' They circle him slowly.

There are no houses here—just an empty stretch of road with a multi-storey car park on one side. 'Westhill.' He tries to walk on, but the leader blocks him.

'Westhill stinks. It's full of crap.'

'Yeah.' Elliot wonders if they'll howl before they pounce. He thinks at least there'll be a song in this. If he lives.

'What's with the guitar?' The leader jerks his head at Elliot's shoulder, almost sniffing. 'You in a band or something?'

Not the guitar. *Please. Please.* Elliot holds himself

square, as if this will balance his voice. 'Been for an audition.'

'What for?'

'Pop band. I think that was it anyway. They didn't say exactly.'

'That's a crap way to get discovered. You should work your way up. Sweat for it.'

Elliot nods. He is sweating. 'Yeah—well, I'll have to. Got no choice. I blew it today.'

'Why—you crap?'

'I guess.' From behind him he can feel a shift in the weight of his guitar bag. One of the gang is sliding the zip.

The leader smiles, eyes narrowing. 'Let's get your baby out of its cradle, and you can play for us. We'll decide if you're crap or not. And I'll do a deal—if I reckon you're OK, we'll let you go.'

A breath of wind gushes through Elliot's jacket. Beneath it his flesh is soft fruit. Easily peeled. Are they carrying knives? A red Volkswagen hums past. An old man, his baggy trousers flopping strangely, cycles by. Won't anybody stop? Can't anybody see? Elliot thinks suddenly that he should stand up for himself. Just to get it over with. He'll pulp a few bruises. They'll mush him to bits. Well, stuff it. He's going to lay the first punch.

Only then there are footsteps running towards him. A hand on his arm. 'There you are. We've been looking everywhere for you. Mum's going mental.'

Elliot turns and Wild Roses is at his shoulder again.

The leader flinches back like a dog from a stone. 'How you doing?' His eyes are on hers, and he's not looking at Elliot any more.

'Good. Brilliant, thanks. You?'

'Yeah. Got a job. Working with my uncle fixing cars.'

'I always knew you'd do well.' She smiles. That honeyed smile.

The leader stares at his trainers. Shuffles his feet.

She links her arm through Elliot's, leads him towards the car park. 'Just keep walking,' she murmurs. 'He's just a geek really. They all are. We'll be OK.'

Elliot walks, incredulous, beside her. He is thinking maybe it's time he started to believe in angels.

You got me trapped.
No good at fighting.
Wild things get let loose in writing.

Chapter Four

Anna can't believe she's caught up with him. He blew her away back at the auditions. She's not even sure why, but she'd kept one eye on the door, waiting for him to come out. And then stupidly, stupidly, she'd been distracted by someone, and the next thing she knew he was gone.

She has his arm and she can feel his warmth through his jacket sleeve. He's gorgeous. Incredible. He probably has two million girlfriends.

'You saved me. From a sticky end.'

'I told you, they're geeks. They used to go to my school. Newton Comp. They were a year above.' She glances at him, trying not to look for too long, as if her looking is stealing something from him. He has an air of quiet, something closed in. A room with the door shut.

They climb the next block of stairs, and then the next. 'We made it. We're at the top.' She throws him a smile, then worries that she's being boring and obvious.

He leans his head against the wall, where angry red graffiti screeches HANNAH HAS CRABS across the roughened bricks.

The stench of urine is stinging.

'Come on.' Anna wants—needs—to feel the cold car park air. 'Let's breathe a bit.'

She bangs ahead of him through the door. The bays are empty, except for an oil-black Mercedes parked by the nearest pillar. The sky floats like a lost world inside its windscreen, and one fire-gold leaf has settled on the bonnet.

They are high high high and the wind spins against them. She follows Elliot, thinking how his hair is all rumpled and wild. Her own hair is doing a mad dance and she presses her hand on top of her denim cap to stop it whisking away. She's sure she looks a mess.

'What's your name?' He is having to shout.

'Anna. Anna Brook,' she shouts back. 'What about yours?'

'I'm Elliot. Elliot Heath.'

They stand stupidly, awkwardly. His eyes are beautiful. A melting brown. Anna feels a skittering in her chest, and a rush of longing to reach forward and touch him. Only lightly—maybe on his hand or his arm. Nothing embarrassing. Nothing he would probably even notice.

She realizes it actually hurts her, just looking at him. Can you feel that way about someone and have the other person just not know? She turns and makes herself walk back towards the stairwell. By the time she's got home and nattered to Mum and they've gone out and fed Silver and cooked and cleared away, this wild need will have died, like a wind dropping.

They reach the door and head down the stairs.

Back just inside the car park entrance, he looks around and suddenly, startlingly, cups his hands round his mouth and hoots.

'What's up?'

'The acoustics in here. They're great.'

She cups her own hands, makes the call. The sound bounces round them, low and deep. She is thinking that she loves it that he's thought of this. Loves it that he isn't embarrassed. Loves it that he's different.

He grins at her then, a tiny chink of him opening up. 'Sorry—I should've asked, how did it go? The audition?'

She wrinkles her nose and shakes her head. 'Rubbish.'

'Me too. I really blew it. I'm gutted now.'

She thinks for a minute. 'I'm not. Gutted, I mean. Mum thought I should go because it was local and she's been throwing money at singing lessons for me, so I went to keep her happy. I wouldn't want to have got chosen. Not really. My dream is to study art. I'll be going to college next year.'

'I'm doing music. Then I'll do teacher training. That's more for my mum than me too. The teaching bit, I mean.'

Anna likes the way he speaks. Everything spare. Just the bones of sentences. Not like her, gushing and rushing and tumbling over ideas.

She realizes then that he's unzipping his guitar case, sliding his back down the wall until he is sitting cross-legged on the floor.

She slides down too, tucking her legs underneath and feeling the cold concrete through her jeans. Is he always like this? It excites her, the strangeness of him. The distance.

He plays a few chords and they tremble in the air. And then he sings.

His voice is gritted and raw, every sound torn. 'Untouchable'. The word a repeated lyric weaving its way through the rhythm.

The song is everything. Anna can taste it. Breathe it. A thin shiver skims her spine. It seems too much to look at him and she stares across at the graffiti-scarred brickwork and thinks that even if she never ever sees him again he will have made a difference. Made her think differently. Made her feel differently.

Neither of them notices the door push open.

Elliot fades out the last line and she grazes a look at him. Nothing she says would be enough. And then she realizes someone is standing beside them.

He looks up at the same moment she does, 'Kris Kowper?' His mouth has dropped open. 'From the auditions?'

Kris Kowper's sharp, watchful face is shaped by an odd expression, as if he has been startled into remembering something he was supposed to do. 'What was your name?' he says.

'Elliot. Elliot Heath.' Elliot pushes himself up to standing. Anna stands too.

'We've got your details, haven't we? You filled in a form?'

'Yeah.' Elliot glances at Anna, as if the full-on attention is uncomfortable for him. 'We both did.'

Kris Kowper doesn't look at Anna. 'Good.' He nods, a brisk decisive movement. 'Great.'

He disappears up the stairs and they have moved and are standing just outside the car park, trying to make out the significance of what he said, when the oil-black Mercedes comes sleeking past them. It is Kris driving. As he pauses by the barrier the fire-gold leaf slides off the bonnet and down on to the concrete. It is crushed by the back tyres as the car spins away.

Chapter Five

Sheldon's Saab convertible is hauled up on the kerb outside Mum's place, parked underneath the tree. Elliot notices the bird droppings on the soft-top roof, and is glad. A second later he is sorry he is glad. He is always like that about Sheldon. He walks up the path and rings the bell.

'Sweetheart. You should've said you were coming. Why didn't you use the key?'

Mum's warm welcome smile wavers as her eyes flick to the guitar over his shoulder. 'Where've you been?'

'To a drug-crazed orgy.' He steps past her, propping his guitar against the wall. The air holds the scent of lemon air freshener, mixed with lazy wafts of roasting meat. Stepping into the kitchen he sees pans bubbling on the cooker.

'How's your dad?' Mum follows him in.

'Fine.'

'Any changes?'

'Only his underpants. I hope.' Elliot can't stop himself, this batting back her questions. Knocking them out of shape. Anyway, the concern is empty. There aren't any changes and she knows there won't be.

Sheldon struts in through the doorway, 'Hey, Elliot. Good to see you. How's things?'

'Fine.'

'Sit down. Get comfortable.' Mum is making tea, and as Sheldon gets down the mugs, Elliot realizes he is dressed like her. Both in navy blue tracksuits. They've probably been out jogging together. He suddenly doesn't want to get comfortable.

'So—how's college?' She brings him the mug, the liquid steaming. Elliot thinks she has gone for the jugular earlier than usual. 'Fine.'

'You must have assessments soon?'

'Yeah.' He sips the tea, gets up to put more milk in it, then sits down again. He wants to be able to drink it faster. He wants to be able to get away.

'Once Christmas is done the time will fly. You need to make sure you're on top of all the revision. You might think you know everything, but there's always that one question that might trip you up. It could make all the difference.' Her eyes burn him. All her needs fired up in the look.

'You're lucky.' Sheldon has his back to Elliot and is standing, legs slightly apart, staring out of the window. The seat of his jogging pants is slightly baggy. 'I never got a decent education. Wish I had. I've had to scratch my way up in PC support. Started off franking envelopes.'

Elliot jiggles the mug, watching the tea lap the edges.

'I wish that too,' says Mum. 'For me, I mean. I

should've gone to college. Things might have been . . .' She stops. Sighs. Runs her hand backwards through her hair.

Elliot thinks that if he jiggles faster, the tea could slop over the side. A stain on the lemon-polished table.

'Your dad's never cared about what I need.' Mum said this once in a voice that was gritted, not long before she left. *'Too busy staring at the stars.'*

Elliot thinks now about a sky full of stars, dazzling down into an empty car park. When they hit the ground they hiss and ping. Soft mounds of silver dust smoulder where they've been. 'I need to get going.' He gets up quickly, the tea only half drunk.

'Stay and eat with us. We can make it stretch, can't we, Sheldon?'

'Sure. Of course.'

'I'm eating with Dad.' There is a silence.

Elliot is glad of the silence in the same way he was glad about the bird droppings. Mum follows him into the hall, watches him pick up his guitar.

'Come by next week, won't you?' She brushes a hair from his jacket as they reach the front door. 'I'll do a Bolognese if you let me know what day.'

'Yeah. Thanks.' The door closes Mum and Sheldon back into their matching tracksuit lives.

The blue day is fading. A fresh fall of leaves has gusted down on to the road and been pressed flat by cars, decorating the tarmac. When he was a kid, Mum used to help him press leaves and make pictures out of them.

Pictures of leaves left crushed on the floor.
She is leaving.
Leaves.
Closing the door.

Chapter Six

There is a moment—a pause—before Dad stumbles out his question, each word heavy and tired, as if there are weights inside them. 'Where've . . . you . . . been?'

Elliot pushes his key back in his pocket and steps past him into the hallway. He had hoped to get upstairs—at least to put the guitar away—but Dad is shuffling about by the front door. He's probably been waiting.

Elliot props the guitar against the wall and heads for the kitchen. 'There's a college gig coming up. For Christmas. Been practising for it.'

'You should've told me.' Dad shadows him, just one step behind. 'We could've talked it through.'

'Yeah. Sorry.' Elliot wishes he hadn't had to mention gigs or practices. But at least he hasn't let on where he's really been.

'I remember the first one *I* did. When I was with Davey and Mo. That was the first band . . . I don't know if I told you this story but . . .' Dad's voice has grown lighter with the memory.

'Yeah, you did. The Heroes. You nearly got a deal but Mo got offered a place at Oxford so he went off to be a politician instead.' Elliot knows every one of

Dad's stories. He can see them stacked up, like old vinyl records, the album sleeves fading and creased. Could've been. Wanna be. Has been. Dad is an album that plays over and over, only the songs are all scratched and no one can bear to listen. Elliot checks Dad's anti-depressants that he left on the side that morning, making sure he's remembered to take them.

He has. Although Elliot isn't always sure they're doing him any good. Some days his head is all over the place.

'I went with Coiled Cobra after that. I can dig out the old video later. Have I shown you that one?'

'Yeah, Dad, you have.' Elliot thinks he's probably watched it about fifty million times. 'But maybe we'll do it again later.' He switches Dad off, picks up the bowl of soggy cornflakes he hadn't been able to face earlier that morning, and scrapes them into the bin. 'Oh sh—!' The bag is full and a thin dribble of milk puddles the rim, sliding slowly down the outside.

Dad plucks at his sleeve, as if he's picking off imaginary fluff. 'You can bring your friends back here to practise if you want. We could soundproof the spare bedroom. Have you got a set list yet?'

'Not yet.' Elliot rinses the bowl under the tap, then opens the window above the sink to let some air in. The kitchen stinks. The whole house does. He can't remember the last time he brought anyone back here.

It is almost dark, smudges of light coming on all over the Westhill Estate. Cosy houses. Sunday people houses. Elliot thinks about Mum and Sheldon and their wafting tang of roast. 'Shall I do dinner?'

There is a short silence, and then Dad jerks his head round as if he has suddenly realized he's been spoken to. 'I'm not hungry. But you cook something if you want.'

Elliot shrugs. They've got some food—decent food—because he shopped in the week, but he can't be bothered to do it just for himself. 'I'll have a sandwich.'

Dad shuffles away into the front room, and Elliot hears the scrape of Dad's guitar being lifted. He braces himself for the plea. The call to 'come through and listen'.

With one ear on Dad, he sorts out the sandwich, piling in cheese and pickle and tomato sauce. The crusts are stale so he eats round them, then drops them in the bin on top of the soggy cornflakes. Then he wrestles with the bag, hoiking it out of the bin to take it outside. It splits near the bottom, a tea bag trail marking a slug line to the door. Wiping his hands on his jeans, Elliot stands in the garden. It's still windy, untidy clouds chasing across the night. The stars stay hidden but the wash from the moon is misted silver behind the rags of grey.

'Come through and listen!'

Elliot blots Dad out and thinks about Kris Kowper. Would someone say that if they didn't mean it? What are the chances of him changing his mind? Losing the form? Finding some other kid in some other car park who he suddenly decides is better. *Please. Please.*

Elliot wants this so much it scares him.

'Elliot—come through and listen!'

He forces himself to go back in. Dad is playing in the dark. Elliot flicks the light on and the room seems startled, as if it's been suddenly woken. He has the sense of shadows hurriedly having to re-arrange themselves. Dad has his eyes shut and his pale hands pluck at the strings. *'We're going up up up . . .'* Dad's voice, when he sings, is thin and reedy. Elliot thinks of frayed elastic. How easily will it snap? *'. . . But up is never worth the coming down . . .'*

He leans his back against the patio door, thinking he should sort the room out. Take out the coffee mugs. Fold the clothes that are draped across the chairs. Chuck out yesterday's newspaper which is scrunched on the floor. Dad has slid into a different lyric. *'Take me as you find me. No need to remind me . . .'*

Elliot flicks the light off again; the shadows sigh and settle back into place. Then he turns, collects his own guitar from the hall, and goes upstairs.

Dad's voice grows muffled and distant.

Up in his room Elliot straightens the bed and then sits on the edge, staring out at the glare of the street-lamp in the road outside. A couple pass by, pressed against each other, the bloke with one arm round the girl's shoulder.

Watching them, Elliot's insides seem to hollow out, and a slow ache seeps in and fills the space.

He unzips his guitar. The song he plays is loud and fast, something he wrote when he couldn't sleep. A song for Insomniacs. He likes the loudness. He likes the speed. It's best to fill every space with sound. Sound—music—is what keeps him from caving in.

He wonders what Kris Kowper is doing now.

Skin itching leg twitching eyes staring thoughts blaring
teeth clenching gut wrenching heart burning bed
turning
can't get no sleep tonight.

NEWTON NEWS

LOCAL NEWS, LOCAL ISSUES

DIGGING UP DREAMS

By Paige Melder

Young hopefuls all over the south flocked to take part in a day of auditions, held yesterday at the Circle Hotel, in Crossford Lane. Kris Kowper (former manager to Declan Barrett, of 'Sabotage') told us, 'Events like this are always exciting. A bit like a treasure hunt. You never know what you're going to dig up.'

'I just hope it's me on the end of his spade,' joked Della Hind, one of the hopefuls, who has performed locally at clubs such as *The Joiners* and *The White Hart* pub.

'I've been trying to break through to the next level for years. I'm good—I know I'm good—but there's just so much competition. If I get through on this, my dream will have come true.'

The event attracted well over 100 candidates and the organisers, Pineapple Promotions, will be contacting those selected over the next few weeks.

Chapter Seven

It is Monday, just over a week later, when the phone call comes.

Dad takes it, fumbling with the receiver as if he's not sure which way up it's supposed to go. 'For you.' He shakes his head, his eyes slightly panicky. The way he gets when the outside world pushes its way into the house.

Elliot has just come in from college. He swings his bag and hooks it on to the banister.

'Hello?'

'Elliot Heath?'

'Yeah.' Elliot knows this voice. Has been waiting to hear it. But now it is here it scares him.

'This is Kris Kowper.'

Elliot pushes his finger into the coiled wire of the phone. He wishes Dad wasn't hovering.

'I've got a couple of ideas—suggestions—that I want to put to you. I might be able to use you for something.'

'Yeah. Sure.' *Use me. Please. Please.*

'I've booked some time at a studio. It's fairly local to you. I'm hooking up with some of the other kids there—those we picked out last Sunday. It would be good if you could get over. Have a bit of a chat.'

'Yeah. Sure. When?'

'It's two weeks Sunday. We've got the studio booked from about ten, but I reckon I'll be done with the others by four. Could you come over then? I need a proper look at you.'

Elliot pictures Kris Kowper walking slowly round him, checking his teeth. 'Sure. Sounds good.'

'It's the Dungeon Studio. D'you know it?'

'I'll find it.'

'Great. Fantastic. Bring your guitar—and I'll see you there.'

'Yeah.'

The line clicks dead and Elliot stays standing, staring at the receiver. He can't put it down. Putting it down will break the moment.

But the moment breaks anyway, with Dad shuffling up again. 'Everything all right?'

'Yeah.'

Elliot sits on the bottom stair, reeling his way back through the conversation, fishing for hidden signs that might hook out what Kris was really thinking. Dad watches him anxiously, rubbing his ear and brushing imaginary fluff off his sleeve. Elliot looks up at him. What's it like when your dream gets squashed? He sees Dad's dream like a lemon yellow butterfly. And Mum's heel on it. Grinding it, grinding it, dust in the carpet. Spitting fury about the mess.

He stands up, puts his hand on Dad's shoulder. 'Everything's OK. Trust me.'

Crush out the screams
Of the butterfly.
Pin your dreams
On me.

Chapter Eight

This time Anna thinks it must be fate, or destiny, that lets her find Elliot again. She sees him straight away as he comes swinging out through the Westhill College doors, down the steps and across the car park.

The sky is swollen, a weighted grey. It has begun to snow. She struggles to get out of the car before he is gone. 'Elliot!'

Her voice stops him. 'Hello?' It is a question, not a greeting. He doesn't remember her. She can see that. She stands awkwardly, stung and stupid. She should have just let him walk by.

'It's Anna. From the audition day.' The snow flakes down on to the dark blue collar of his jacket. She wants to brush it away.

There is another moment—a second—a lifetime—when his eyes just search, and then he smiles. 'Hi. What you doing here?'

She had remembered lots of things about him, but she had forgotten his voice. The raw edge of it. The depth. 'I'm here to look round. This is my mum. We missed Open Evening because we were in Italy, so they said we could come now. Before they break up. I didn't know you came here.'

'I'm in my first year. Studying music mainly.'

'I know.' She bites at her bottom lip. She shouldn't have let on that every detail of the things he said has stayed pressed in her. 'Mum—this is Elliot. He went to that audition the other week.'

Anna's mum shuts the car door, clicks the lock, and walks over. 'Hi, Elliot. Good to see you.' Anna is glad Mum went for the beige suit instead of the usual smelly jodhpurs and jacket.

The three of them stand, the snow now whirling a mad dance, sheeting one way and then another.

Anna thinks she has to come up with something to say. 'I love this weather. It makes everything so strange. But it's early in the year, isn't it? For snow, I mean.'

'Yeah.' Elliot looks up at the sky as if he has noticed the blizzard for the first time.

Anna feels a flake burn her cheek. 'Did you hear anything? From that audition bloke, I mean?'

'Yeah. I'm seeing him. Next Sunday.'

'Oh—brilliant. Well done. That's amazing.' She's gushing. Spilling. She wants to give him a hug.

A girl walks across the car park, slows her steps as she passes. Stops and watches. She has red-brown hair that seems to burn fire against all the greys and whites. Elliot glances round at her, nods, and turns away again. The girl brushes a look at Anna then walks on, the fine points of her heels making a dotted line across the icing of snow.

'Sweetheart—we're running late. We were supposed

to be meeting the college principal about two minutes ago.' Mum is moving away towards the building.

'Yeah. OK.' Anna thinks that this is it. It's all about to finish. The snow lays kisses in his hair. 'Could you . . . would you let me know? How you get on?'

'Give me your number.' He pulls his mobile out of his pocket. 'I'll text you.'

'Anna—please.' Mum has reached the steps that lead up to the main entrance. Her voice as she calls as insistent as a buzzer.

Anna gabbles out, '08797 628580.'

He blows snow from his mobile, then punches the number in.

'Anna—come ON!'

Elliot nods, raises one hand, and dips towards her slightly. 'Sorry. I've got you in trouble. I'd better go.' He walks on.

Anna hurries to catch up with Mum. Her feet slip, and she has to steady herself like a failing ballerina. She hopes he's not watching. She hopes hopes hopes he'll ring. As she reaches the steps she turns, picking out the dark shape that is him leaving. He isn't watching. Of course not. Why would he?

She wonders what the point was of that—fate and destiny giving her just a scratch of him, and then snatching him away again. She notices his footprints have crossed over those of the fire-haired girl, and Anna's own have crossed over both of them, patterning a strangely shaped star into the deepening snow.

NEWTON NEWS

LOCAL NEWS, LOCAL ISSUES

STARS IN THEIR EYES

By Paige Melder

Following our report on the queues of young hopefuls who recently auditioned for the promise of stardom at a Newton hotel, Kris Kowper, one of the production team involved in the project, tells us he has narrowed the search down to a 'possible 5' singers.

'We're after a package. We've got the song and we've got the sound,' he said, 'but it's a much harder job trying to find the personalities who can be moulded to the market we are targeting. It's a tough, rough world, and we need to be confident we're only going to put money into those who have a chance.'

Chapter Nine

The bus pulls away and Elliot stands on the kerb, checking the scrawled map he got from a bloke at college.

Two roads down, first left, then right.

It's cold, and he pulls at his collar as he walks. He feels every step. Counts them. A hundred and three. A hundred and four. How many chances do you get in life? A hundred and eleven. A hundred and twelve.

And there is the sign, an arrow pointing through a gateway. The Dungeon. A red-bricked tunnel. Kris Kowper's black Mercedes parked in the yard. One hundred and nineteen and he is at the door.

There is no bell, and the door isn't locked, so Elliot steps cautiously inside to a clutter of speakers and amps and microphones. It's damp. Not what he expected. A sign on the curving brick wall says *'Go Home and Sleep'*.

'Hey.' A skinny girl swings in through another archway. 'I'm Sophie. Can I help?'

Elliot thinks he recognizes her from the audition day. He's sure she was the anorexic-looking one on the desk, giving out the application forms.

'I'm after Kris Kowper.'

Sophie smiles, her face all teeth and cheekbones.

'They all are, today.'

Elliot feels a sudden stab at the word 'all'. 'All' is too many. 'All' is competition. 'I'm Elliot. Elliot Heath.'

She slants her eyes at him as if she's reading his face, then smiles again. 'OK, Elliot Heath. Follow me.'

As they cross into another tunnelled room, Elliot notices crystals clustered on the ceiling and walls. That damp again. He remembers a cave Dad took him to once, as part of a tour they did one holiday, when everyone was still trying to play 'Happy Families'. He must have been about eight. There were crystals in that cave too, and stalagmites and stalactites and the slow drip drip drip of water. It was the first time he had ever thought about life and death—that drip drip drip going on before he came and after he was gone. He'd got the desperate need then to make a mark—a sign that he'd been there. Hanging back from the tour group, he'd scratched the edge of a coin against the hard wall of rock. 'Elliot'.

Sophie touches his arm, 'That's Rick—the Dungeon manager and sound engineer. Those four with him are Best Cellars. A local band. Some American producer's just offered them a deal.' At one end of the room a group are hunched around a mixing desk. A guy with a shaved head looks up and nods at Sophie, adjusting his headphones.

The band is listening to a heavy guitar riff, playing it over and over and over again.

'A bit more weight,' one of them says.

'And darker. Dirty it up a bit,' says another.

The guitar riff bursts through with a harder edge.

Elliot feels something move through him. A rush of excitement.

Sophie flicks a look at Elliot. 'You not been here before?'

'No.'

From somewhere deeper in the belly of the building another thrum of music is pounding out.

'It's actually an old fort. Victorian. All these tunnels do amazing things for acoustics.'

The room they pass into has foam and bits of old carpet nailed everywhere. 'One of the rehearsal rooms,' says Sophie.

Elliot's gut is starting to churn. His big chance. His one chance. He tries to take his mind off the moment. 'So—do you work here?'

'I work for Kris. As an assistant. Sort of. I was a model but I got really depressed—the other girls were so bitchy and it made me—well, ill.' She clasps her bone-thin fingers together suddenly, almost as if she's praying, and then shrugs. 'So anyway, that's all behind me. I'm trying to learn the music business instead now. I want to get into the make-up side of it. Kris is backing me up. He's good like that, if he thinks you're worth putting time into, then he'll do it. He seems a bit hard sometimes, but that's OK. He has to be.'

Elliot thinks he should answer, croak out something vaguely intelligent. But before he can pull anything from his mind, another door opens and two guys and a girl walk through. One of them is Dreadlocks. He recognizes the girl too. She does the pub circuit. He's seen her in the White Hart quite a bit, when he used to go there with Amber. A good singer. He can't remember her name.

'OK?' Sophie smiles at them all and they hang round near the door as if they're reluctant to leave. Elliot remembers how he felt when he couldn't put down the phone.

'We're waiting for Kris . . .' The girl looks hot and tired. Mascara has smudged under her eyes and her hair is damp and straggled. '. . . he might want to get us to do a bit more.'

And then Kris is there, walking out from the studio. He smiles. 'OK, kids—that was great. Fantastic. I'll be running through it all over the next couple of days, and I'll be back in touch.'

The three of them flash smiles back, but their eyes are raw hunger. Elliot can see it: hope chewing at them. No one wants to be spat back out.

Sophie touches Kris's arm. 'Kris—this is Elliot. He says you're expecting him.'

Kris runs his hand through his hair. 'Hi there. Thanks for coming.' He turns to Sophie. 'Get us a coffee, sweetheart. I need the buzz.' He nudges Elliot. 'Come on through. Let's get moving on this.'

The studio is smaller than the other rooms. More carpet and foam. A whole Persian rug nailed along one wall. Elliot gets out his guitar and Kris pulls up a chair and a mike. 'Just sing. Really go for it. The way you did in that car park.'

'Can I do my own stuff? Songs I've written myself?'

'Anything you like. Mix it up if you want. I need to hear the overall sound.'

Elliot runs through Marc Wild's 'Never Going Home'. Then he spins into 'A Song for Insomniacs'. Tries wild and weird. Then mild and mellow. He closes his eyes as he sings, the coin-scratched 'Elliot' coming back in his head. To be known. To be noticed. The eternal sound of the drip drip drip.

Sophie appears with the coffee, and Kris clicks his fingers for Elliot to stop. 'Thanks, sweetheart.' He winks at her. 'What d'you reckon on this guy?'

Sophie nods. 'He's good. The best from today. In fact—out of everyone we've heard.'

'You've got an ear for quality. You need that. To survive.'

Kris knocks back the coffee, looking at Elliot over the rim of the mug. 'This kid made the hairs stand up on the back of my neck the other week. I don't get that feeling too often.'

Elliot drinks in what he's just heard. If he was a character in a book, he'd pinch himself.

'Do me that one you did in the car park. "Don't touch me"—or whatever it was.'

Elliot is impressed that Kris has remembered a bit of the lyric. '"Untouchable",' he mumbles. 'It's one of my own.'

He closes his eyes, lets the song run through him.

He daren't look at Kris. He daren't let the tremble in his gut reach his voice. This is his chance. His one big chance. *Please. Please.*

'OK, that'll do, I reckon I've got enough.' Kris stops him halfway through.

Elliot's eyes jerk open, trying to read the mood on Kris's face. He seems closed. Inscrutable. Turning away he hands Sophie the mug. 'Pack up now. I'll be in touch.' He gives Elliot one last sharp, brisk nod and is gone.

'Be in touch?' Elliot blinks after him, then swings his guitar over his shoulder. 'Is that good or bad?'

Sophie shrugs as she leads him back to the door. 'He doesn't take on many, but he never stops looking. He knows what he wants. He calls it the next big thing. But it's not easy. Most of the performers you've met here today—even that band—you'll never hear of again.'

Elliot walks back out into the yard and heads for the bus stop. He is thinking of Kris searching the streets. Listening to buskers. Dreamers singing along to their Walkmans. Failed auditionees droning in car parks.

Scratch at chances.
Sing the pain.
Don't leave me
In the cold again.

NEWTON NEWS

LOCAL NEWS, LOCAL ISSUES

HOPES DASHED FOR LOCAL HOPEFULS

Our follow-up report on the five young hopefuls who were plucked from a recent audition has revealed that the production company has yet to find the combination of people who can take their ideas into the starry land of pop. Those shortlisted need not be disappointed, stressed Kris Kowper, one of the team involved in the project. It is a credit to them that they have come this far.

The hopefuls were not so easily comforted. 'I'm gutted,' admitted Gary Wakes, of Hedge Road, when we rang him at home to see how he'd got on. 'Music is my life. It's all I want to do. I'll be writing to Kris to see if he'll give me another try.'

Della Hind, who also made it through to the select five, told us, 'This was a big opportunity. You don't get breaks like this very often. I've been doing the pub and club scene for a couple of years, and there are masses of people desperate to break through. In some ways it's good to have come this far, but in some it's worse. I keep thinking . . . if only I'd tried a bit harder. Sung louder. Or softer . . .'

There is, however, one thin silver lining shining through all these dark clouds. Kris Kowper believes he may have found someone who wouldn't have worked with a group, but has a quality that might pull him through as an individual act . . . Kris is staying tight-lipped about the details, but assures us that if the youngster—who comes from Westhill—can convince him he's 'got what it takes', he'll be pushing him as hard as he can to get him to the next stage.

By Newton News reporter:
Paige Melder

Chapter Ten

Anna is in her room, Boris lying on the floor in front of her bed. She is trying to paint him, her brush chasing the thin spiked lines of his shaggy coat across the paper. Painting stops her panicking.

Boris gazes up at her with warm chocolate eyes and thumps his tail. 'Keep still, Boris. How can I do this if you keep moving?'

Another bus rumbles by. That's three now. Did she give him detailed enough directions? Has he got off at the wrong stop?

From downstairs, she hears a knock on the door. Boris springs up, barking.

Anna pushes the paint things into the corner, muddling up the room she's spent all afternoon tidying. As she squirts herself with Vanilla Body Spray to try and drown out 'Odour of Boris', she panics that her boy band posters might make her seem too young. She should've taken them down. Some of them she doesn't even *like* any more. And the 'Ghosted Girl' self-portrait that Mum had framed—an experiment using really weak water colours—that's a bit pretentious, isn't it? Oh God. Oh God. She's never ever worried about these things before.

Boris lumbers out in front of her, and she hurries down the stairs.

Will he think they've overdone the Christmas decorations? She and Mum like colour. Everything wild.

She can see the blurred blues of his jacket through the ridged glass.

'Hi. You found it OK?'

Stupid question. Of course he did, otherwise he wouldn't be standing there.

'Yeah. No problem.'

Boris is leaping on him, small yelping noises in his throat. She grips his collar, glad of the distraction. 'Sorry. I have to hang on to him or he might go racing out into the traffic. He's not exactly the Einstein of the dog world. Come in.'

He's here, at her house. Oh God. Oh God.

'Hi, Elliot—good to see you again.' Mum appears, still in her jodhpurs and with straw in her hair.

'Hi.'

'We can go upstairs.' Anna is gabbling, hanging his jacket over Silver's saddle, and then wishing she hadn't. It'll get covered in white Silver hairs. He'll spend the next six months hating her as he tries to clean them off. She picks his jacket up again. 'Mum—can you stick this in the kitchen?'

'Of course.' Mum is hovering. 'Are you staying for something to eat? Spaghetti Bolognese?'

Oh no. God no no no. The embarrassment of spaghetti in front of him. 'Can't we have rice?'

'But you love spaghetti.'

'Spaghetti's great.' Elliot is looking from one to the other as if he's not sure what might be the right thing to say.

Anna pushes the image of slurping spaghetti out of her head. 'I've got a telly in my room, and I thought we'd try and catch *Top of the Pops*. Is that OK, Mum?'

'As long as Elliot can bear the mess.'

Anna glares at her. Apart from the paint things, the room is spotless now, but she doesn't want Elliot thinking she tidied it just for him. 'Come on,' she says.

Upstairs they both sit awkwardly on the floor, their backs against her bed. Boris sniffs all round Elliot, then plonks down next to him. Dog hairs. Horse hairs. Spaghetti sauce stains. At least he won't be able to forget her too easily.

She flicks on the screen. 'I don't normally watch this. Telly, I mean. I usually listen to music, and draw.'

'This Traci Maran?'

'Yeah. She was in all the magazines about a month ago.'

Elliot leans forward slightly. 'I bet this makes the Christmas Number One. D'you reckon she's good?'

Anna shrugs, but uncertainty seeps into her. He's looking too interested. If you were with a bloke like Elliot—really with him—you'd want to keep girls like Traci away. She tries to keep her voice light. 'Trouble is, you get so used to hearing all the hype. It's hard to decide.'

'She's only my age.'

'She's a different style to you though. More sort of . . .' she hesitates, '. . . glitzy. And your lyrics are fantastic. That song you sang in the carpark. *Untouchable*. It made me go all shivery when I heard it.' Anna worries that she's said too much, but he just shrugs and shakes his head.

'I can't write at the moment. Since the audition. Nothing's coming. I scribble stuff down but it doesn't take shape.' Elliot's foot taps on the floor, as if there's an energy in him that has become blocked up and needs shaking out. 'I need to work harder. Spend more time on it.' There is a tightness to his voice. Almost a choke.

Anna wonders if she's taking up his time. Probably he regrets coming. It was a spur of the moment thing that they set up when he sent her that text. 'Maybe it's best not to think about it too hard. Distract yourself somehow, and just believe it will suddenly happen—the song, I mean. It'll just come through on its own. That's what I do when I get stuck on a painting. It's sort of a trust thing.' She knows this reply is gabbled. Mangled. He'll probably think she's nuts.

He glances sideways at her—just half a look. Then he rubs the back of his neck. 'Yeah,' he says slowly. 'Maybe.'

Oh God. Oh God. What does 'maybe' mean. What's he *really* thinking?

Traci Maran fades out to a roar of applause, and

Craig Harris is interviewing Jason Kaye, from the Sessions. Anna imagines Elliot there. His face on the screen. She knows she's going to start gabbling again, but she can't stop herself. She wants to keep talking to him. And she wants him to keep talking to her. 'Have you ever dreamed of being on telly? Thought what you'd say in all the interviews? Your likes and dislikes. Who you're influenced by? Your favourite sweets? All that sort of rubbish they always get asked.'

'Favourite sweets?' He looks at her, a proper look, as if the question actually matters. 'I'd go for curly-whirly toffees.'

Anna feels goosebumps prickle through her. Gorgeous gorgeous gorgeous. He has his own smell. Slightly musky. She read somewhere once that people are attracted to each other by smell. It's a secret code and you don't even know it's happening. Except she does. She knows it's happening. She feels dizzy, almost drunk, with the closeness of him. Say something normal. Say something normal. 'I'd choose Smarties. The orange ones. I always pick them out and save them for when I want to give myself a lift.'

'Oh yeah—I like them too.'

'Green triangles in Quality Street.'

He nods. 'Liquorice Allsorts with those dots all over them.'

Craig Harris steps back from Jason Kaye. 'And now we've got a video for you—one of the best girl bands around—Heaven Scent . . .'

Anna gets up and goes over to her dressing table,

riffles through the bottom drawer, then turns to Elliot. 'Close your eyes.'

The look he gives her is full on then and she thinks, if he ever looked like that on screen, on somewhere like *Top of the Pops*, a million girls all over the world would melt. It would be in all the papers. A mass melting of girls. A new and terrifying phenomenon.

He closes his eyes.

'Hold out your hand.' Anna was going to tell him to open his mouth but it feels too forward. Too much like a come on. She's not coming on to him. She wouldn't stand a chance. 'Here. You can open your eyes now.'

He looks down at the single orange Smartie that she has pressed on to his palm. 'Thanks.' He has a slow smile. Careful. Uncertain. But when it reaches his eyes, he's full of light. A warmth round him.

She suddenly wants to tell him he can have all her favourites. All the orange Smarties and green triangles and Liquorice Allsorts with those dots all over them that she can find. But she doesn't say it. It would be too much. 'Eat it,' she says. 'Or it'll melt.'

He knocks it into his mouth, pressing his open palm against his face. 'Thanks.' That smile again.

She flicks off the telly.

Outside another bus rattles by.

He is so beautiful that it hurts.

Chapter Eleven

Elliot walks away down the road. He'll pick up a bus a couple of stops along. He needs to walk. Watching that *Top of the Pops* has got under his skin. It's always like that when he sees other bands or singers. It makes him restless. Edgy. He wants to be where they are. And he wants to be there now.

Please. Please.

Anna said he had to distract himself, and he knows she's right. He likes her. Not just the way she looks, but the things she says. He's not used to that—girls he can talk to. Girls saying stuff that seems to hook into the way he thinks. It was never like that with Amber.

There's a newsagent on the corner of the road, and he pushes in through the door. He wants to pick up one of the music papers—*Music and Blues,* if they've got it. They keep up with a lot of new stuff. But it isn't there, just a few of the cheap tabloids grubbing up the shelves.

'I help you?'

Elliot realizes that the shopkeeper is watching him with the eyes of someone who has learnt to be suspicious of young blokes in scruffy jackets. He scans the shop. There must be *something* in here that he wants.

The back shelves are lined with sweet jars—the old-fashioned sort. All colours. All types. Pastel soft marsh-mallows. Gold crunch peanut toffees. Chocolates in brassy bright foil.

He stands, his eyes locked on to them for a moment, and as he stares, a line comes into his head. A new lyric. A new rhythm. He scrabbles in his pocket, pulls out his notebook. *A sort of trust thing.* His mind dances out words. The tune. He could almost sing it standing here.

'There is problem?' The man shuffles nervously, eyeing the notebook. Elliot realizes he probably thinks he's an inspector or something, disguised as a yob. The song still fizzes through him, like something spilling. 'Sorry, mate—I . . .' His eyes rove the shelves desperately. Quality Street. A whole jar of green ones. That was what Anna said she liked. 'Hey, mate.' Elliot nods at the jar. 'Those please. Just fill me the biggest bag you've got.'

A minute later he leaves the shop, the bag bulging in his pocket, still scribbling in his book.

Anna was right. He got distracted, and the song just came. It came because she made him believe it would. A sort of trust thing.

Retracing his steps back to her house, he pushes the bag through the letter box and hurries away before anyone comes to the door. He hasn't got time to stop and talk. It's just a thank you.

But he could do with someone like her around more often.

A sort of trust thing
taught my soul
to sing.

Chapter Twelve

'Yes?' The man peers nervously round the edge of the door.

Kris Kowper puts down his briefcase and holds out his hand. 'Mr Heath? Elliot's dad?'

The tired dark eyes—Elliot's, but not quite—stare at the hand and widen in startled panic. He's a small man. Stooped. Hollowed out. Kris thinks there is the shadow of a resemblance, but Elliot must have got most of his looks from his mum. He drops his hand back to his side.

Elliot's dad opens the door slightly wider. 'Is he in trouble?'

'No—not at all.' Kris is all smiles. Soothing. 'My name's Kris Kowper.'

Elliot's dad blinks. Looks nervously over Kris's shoulder. 'Who?'

Kris is knocked back by the question. Parents usually know his name. They've usually been waiting, hanging on the edge of their dreams, for news. 'Elliot came to the studio for me last week. After the audition. We made a demo.' He finds himself speaking slowly, the way you'd talk to a small child.

'Audition? A demo?' Elliot's dad blinks again. 'Elliot made a demo?'

'Is he in?' Kris is wishing now that he'd rung, but the cold call always gives him a chance to get a bit of insight. See people's lives in the raw. It helps him pitch things for each individual kid.

'No . . . but . . .' Elliot's dad seems to draw himself up, as if he's physically struggling to hold himself together. 'A demo?'

'I'm a manager.' Kris flashes a card from his pocket. 'I reckon Elliot's got talent. I'm here to tell him something good.'

'Something good?' Elliot's dad squints down at the card, then looks at Kris properly for the first time, everything about him suddenly strengthened. 'I know the music scene. You'd better fill me in on what's going on. Better help him.' His voice drops to a mutter. 'Got to be there for your own son. He's made a demo. This man's a manager.'

He still doesn't move.

'I'm a normal bloke too though,' Kris hurries to add this. 'Wife and two kids. They live further south—a place in the country. I work in London. Got an apartment up there. Well, several actually. Get back home whenever I can, though it's a struggle sometimes. Trying to keep everyone happy.'

It's this last sentence that seems to do it. Elliot's dad begins nodding fiercely. 'Can be a struggle that. Keeping everyone happy.'

'You're telling me.' Kris raises his eyebrows, shakes his head and shrugs, a silent message to Elliot's dad that the business of keeping everyone happy is beyond his capability. But he tries. The bloke seems shot away, but if Kris can get him to latch on to a common bond it'll help the whole process. Basic psychology. And signing kids up is a serious business.

Minutes later Kris is sitting in the muddled front room, a mug of warm tea in his hand. The curtains are still drawn, and there are stains on the walls. No Christmas decorations. Just a few cards strung out on a faded yellow ribbon. He should've pictured a backdrop like this. That pain in the kid's voice. The wrench in his playing. Great stuff grows from things that hurt. He's seen that so many times before.

'I can't believe he didn't tell me.' Elliot's dad plucks at something invisible on his jumper. 'You'd have thought he would. I know the music scene.'

Kris scans the room, putting the kid's life together in his head. No sign of a woman. A mother. That might be a good thing. Mother's are usually over-ambitious or over-protective. He's had trouble from mothers before. 'Teenagers,' he says out loud. 'Secrecy is part of the game.'

Elliot's dad rubs both hands across his cheeks. 'He's always been like that. A quiet kid. My wife—ex-wife—used to call him "untouchable".'

The last word stings into Kris like an arrow. Untouchable. It's the strongest number on the demo—will probably make it as a single. But it's bigger than that. They could build a whole image round it. He hasn't come up with a theme for Elliot yet—a brand

—and the quicker they get something running, the better.

'I'm a musician too.' Elliot's dad starts nodding his head as he walks over to a drawer and pulls out some old newspapers. 'That's me. Look.'

Kris smiles his soothing smile as he takes the yellowed cutting. If he had a quid for everyone who tells him they're a musician . . . The bloke in the picture looks about twenty. Wiry. Punky. A bit off the wall. He's waving a guitar and the caption reads 'ALL THE WAY UP'. Something about Billy Heath and a single he's bringing out. There isn't time to read it, though, because Elliot's dad, who has been reading the cutting over his shoulder, jolts backwards. 'He's coming.'

The dad's ears are sharper than a dog's. Kris gets the idea he spends all day waiting for that key in the lock. He watches him shuffle into the hall. Hears the mumbled exchange. Sees the back of Elliot as he hooks his bag over the banister.

'I can't believe you didn't tell me,' Billy Heath is saying, as he follows Elliot into the room.

'Hi.' Elliot stands awkwardly just inside the doorway.

Kris clicks a look at him. How will he look on an album cover? On stage? On telly?

'Hi.' He leans forward from the armchair, stretches his hand. 'I'm sorry about just appearing, but I was in the area and I was pretty keyed up about you. The demo was fantastic. I've got it with me.' He unclips his briefcase and brings the CD out, along with a brown manila envelope.

Billy Heath steps forward. 'Elliot's demo?'

Kris sees Elliot glance at him, and then away. He's holding stuff in. He can see that now. It's good. It's good. All that creative angst. And then there are his looks. He's seen plain kids do well with a genius talent. He's seen fantastic looking kids do well, with no talent at all. But this one . . . this one . . .

Billy Heath's hands are shaking as he takes the demo from him. 'Can we hear it?'

'Sure.' Kris smiles at Elliot, to let him know he's on his side. He will be someone strong behind him. And at least the dad doesn't look as if he's up to interfering. The guitar intro curls into the room, Elliot's voice kicks in, bleeding sound. His whole soul in the lyrics. 'Untouchable'.

Kris watches him for reactions. It's hard to tell. The kid's way down deep inside himself. Just like the song is saying. 'I've added a bit more backing. Given the whole thing a darker edge. But it didn't need much. Most of it's already there.'

'Untouchable' fades, and the next track starts up.

Billy Heath is nodding, tapping his knee with his hand. He's out of time. A second behind. As if he's tuned into a different beat.

'Sit down.' Kris holds out the envelope. 'We'll look over the contract together.'

Elliot sits on the chair opposite, and Kris hands the envelope to him.

'Does he have to sign it now?' The dad puts his hand to his ear, flapping at it, as if an insect has suddenly buzzed by.

'I just talk you through it today. I recommend you take it to a solicitor—someone of your own choice—and get it checked through.' He turns back to Elliot. 'I'm offering a minimum two year plan. Provided you work out, I see you as a long term project.'

'A project?' Elliot looks puzzled.

'I'll be putting together a package.'

'What does that mean?'

'You're a product. The way you look. The way you sound. That's all one part of it. And then there's the marketing. The way we get people to think about you. The image they carry round with them.'

'What do I have to do?'

'Once we've agreed that you're up for it, I'll be arranging for you to do a photo shoot. I'll need to send pics up to a few of the majors. And then, if anyone bites, the whole machine can start rolling.'

'You mean gigs and stuff?'

'That's the beginning. But I'm already thinking ahead. The music's not enough on its own these days. We need the whole package. T-shirts. Caps. Badges. If kids have got your poster on their wall, and your T-shirt in their wardrobe, then they're in the fan club. They've bought into you, and that's loyalty. They won't let you down—unless you do the dirty on them.'

'What d'you mean?'

'You live up to the image. You be all the things they need you to be.'

'What like?'

Kris smiles. 'With you, it'll mainly be a female following. That's who we'll be targeting. We want them all to fall in love with you.'

'But the music? That's in it too, isn't it? Blokes'll like my music?'

'Sure. Sure.' Kris nods quickly. And it's true anyway. Some will. But not enough. He won't be able to get the same sort of frenzy going among the boys.

'So—how do you see me coming across?'

Kris runs his eyes over Elliot, as if he's considering it, but over the last half hour his ideas have already been setting in. People want what they can't have—especially girls. So they build Elliot up as a sex god, and then plaster an untouchable sticker on his head. Half the female population in the land will see it as their personal quest to tear it off. To be the one that breaks through to the 'real Elliot'.

'Untouchable,' he says.

'What?'

Kris gives Elliot a long look. 'Just have a read through that contract for now. And trust me.' He's kept his voice cool, but inside the adrenalin is boiling. He can't wait to start putting the Elliot machine together.

Westhill Weekly

THAT SPECIAL SOMETHING

Local music student Elliot Heath has been picked from a recent audition by manager Kris Kowper.
'Elliot has really got something,' Kris told our reporter. 'Not just the looks but the whole sound. A complete package.'
Elliot, 18, who says he has only played 'college gigs' before, has just been booked to support *Sabotage* — the Dublin-based band who are touring Britain over the next few months.

The venue is The Edge, box office 01476 556667 or online from www.the-edge.co.uk

Patty Gilhooly

Chapter Thirteen

Amber sees them all hanging round him in the canteen, and feels the prickling under her skin that starts when someone she's been out with is coming on to someone else. Not that Elliot looks as if he's coming on to anyone particularly. If anything, he looks as if he'd like to get away. It's them—Sally and Melissa and Louise—all dripping over *him*.

She's sure it's no accident that they've picked out the table under the mistletoe. Sally and Louise have silly bits of tinsel in their hair. They're her age, but so boringly young. And so irritating.

She walks near, making it look as if she's just about to pass and then suddenly changes her mind. 'Hi, you lot. What's up?'

'It's Elliot. He was in this yesterday.' Melissa waves a newspaper in Amber's face. 'Didn't you see?'

'I was out. What you done? Robbed a bank?' She flashes a look that dances out to meet Elliot's. She always enjoyed that, looking straight at him, deep into him. It wasn't till the end, just before she dumped him, that he started giving her that sort of look back. But he looks different today, and that pricks at her too. 'Your hair . . .' She keeps her face smiling. 'What happened?'

'He had to have a photo shoot. His manager got a make-up girl to plan the whole look. An ex-model. Go on—read it.' Sally is gushing like a toilet.

Amber already hates the ex-model make-up girl as she takes the newspaper. Is Elliot too wimpy to plan his own 'look'?

But he doesn't *look* wimpy. His face in the photograph stares past her, as if he is seeing a different future. A better one. She prickles again.

'He looks gorgeous, doesn't he?' Sally leans over her shoulder, twizzling a ratty strand of dyed blonde hair round and round her finger. She reeks of cheap perfume.

'Mysterious.' Melissa rolls the word round her mouth. 'I love mysterious guys.'

Amber flicks a glance at them, then skims the article. 'So you've been discovered.' She smiles across at Elliot, her warmest smile, her eyes still dancing. 'You always dreamt of that. I can remember you telling me.' She slips the last bit in, making her point to the others. She went out with him. He whispered his dreams to her.

'I'll get you another coffee,' purrs Louise, touching Elliot's shoulder.

'Oh—buy him a double chocolate muffin. From me,' adds Melissa.

'It's OK.' Elliot speaks for the first time. 'I'm not hungry.'

'You need to eat. You'll need all your strength and energy if you're going to perform in front of thousands.' Louise has kept her hand on his shoulder. Amber thinks she should take more care of her nails if she's going to flaunt them like that.

'And we need to look after you. We could become your groupies.' Sally giggles.

Louise giggles too. 'We'll follow you to America.'

'The world.' Melissa is looking as if she'd happily jump off the edge of the planet with him.

Amber steps back, wanting to slice herself off from them. Wanting Elliot to see that she's not part of this simpering fan club. Rule number 1: never let a bloke see that you're interested.

'We should all go,' she says brightly, as Louise turns away and heads to the food counter. 'To the gig, I mean.'

'Can you get us in free? On the guest list?' Melissa presses her palms together as if she is praying.

'I dunno.' Elliot shakes his head. 'It's my first time. I don't really know how it all works.'

'It's OK, we don't want freebies.' Amber pulls a chair round the wrong way and sits astride it, resting her arms on the back. She's got her hair loose today, and she's glad. Elliot used to touch it and run his fingers through it. Fox-red, he'd whispered. She'd liked the image. A foxy lady. Wild. Untamed. They'd had a good time together really. Funny how easy it is to forget. She skims a melting look at him, to show him she knows that he's suffering. She understands him. She raises her eyebrows and looks at Melissa.'If we're *true* friends we should pay for our tickets. That way the venue makes a profit, and they book Elliot again.'

Melissa flushes pink. 'I know. I was only joking.'

Louise comes back with the coffee and a muffin, sliding Elliot's on to the table. 'Eat.' Her chair seems to have edged closer to his. Any minute now and she'll be sitting on his lap. 'I can design you a web site.' She flicks her short frizz of curls back from her face. 'I'll make it part of my IT assignment.'

Amber's glad Louise has got hair like that. Louise is the best looking out of the three, but there's no way Elliot would go for a frizzer.

He has a mouth full of muffin and has to swallow before he can answer. 'It's OK. My manager's getting that sorted.'

'Oooooh, sweetie!' Louise and Sally lean together and giggle. 'My *manager*.'

Melissa stretches across and breaks off a piece of muffin. For one terrible minute Amber thinks she's going to try and feed it to Elliot, but she stuffs it into her own mouth. 'You don't mind do you?' She hunches her shoulders at him as if she is sharing secrets. 'I couldn't afford two.'

Amber looks away, struggling not to roll her eyes. Across the room she sees Rory come in. She looks back at Elliot quickly, hoping Rory won't notice her, but he races over. She'd been trying to hook Rory for a while. She thought a second year student, and specially one who was leader of the union, would be good for her. She likes blokes with a bit of power.

But now, just the sight of him bores her.

Rory lays an arm along her shoulder. She stiffens slightly, hoping he can feel the freeze. Probably not. In her experience blokes need subtle hints battered in with a sledgehammer. Keeping her gaze on Elliot she says, 'Elliot's at The Edge soon. Could you organize publicity for him. Posters and stuff?'

'Yeah.' Rory strokes her arm and tries to nibble her ear.

She moves her arm away. She scratched her wrists again, last week when she had that row with Mum, and she doesn't want to draw attention to them.

Rory has another try at the ear. 'Who's Elliot?'

'The bloke sitting opposite you. He's got a gig. Supporting Sabotage.' She tilts her head away slightly.

'Sabotage?' Rory jerks a nod at Elliot and sends him a thumbs-up sign. 'They're good. The lead singer is that Declan . . .'

Amber cuts in before Rory launches off on some boring biography of whoever the lead singer is. 'And what about using the college mini-van to get a group of us up there. You could drive us. It could be an end of term Christmas outing.'

'Yeah.' He makes a last ditch play for her ear, and this time she lets him. But it's Elliot she's smiling at, a wide, open smile. She doesn't use those sorts of smiles too often. She wouldn't want to waste them.

It's not wasted on Elliot today though. He glances up at her and then away. He has beautiful eyes. Dark unreadable sexy eyes. She'd forgotten that too.

'I need to get going,' she says. Rule number 2: always be the first to leave. And rule number 3: make sure you sound busy and important. 'I've got stacks to do. See you all around.'

She holds Elliot's gaze for just a moment more before she shakes free from Rory and swings away across the canteen.

She knows Elliot's watching her. He's bound to be.

Blokes are fun. All this sort of stuff is fun. If only it wasn't so easy.

Chapter Fourteen

'I don't really know you, do I?' Anna says this quietly. So quietly, there is a chance Elliot might not hear.

'What d'you mean?'

She frowns down at the shallow stream where the ducks squabble noisily, stirring up the fringes of reeds. 'It's just . . .' she bends to pick up a stick, snapping it in half, spinning the two pieces down beneath the bridge that they're standing on, '. . . you never talk about your family or friends. I don't even know where you live.'

'There's a bunch of mates I hang around with at college—musicians mainly—but no one special.'

The twigs separate, journeying away. 'Your family then. Do you get on with them?'

There is a moment before he answers. 'Live with my dad. Mum left.'

'I'm sorry.' Anna keeps her eyes on the water. A small silver fish darts out from the weeds, then dives back in again. 'Do you still see her?'

'Yep.' He turns from the stream and begins walking towards the swings. Boris thunders past, chasing a small brown collie.

'So—do you get on OK with your dad?' Anna's

voice is careful. Hesitant. Bare feet on shingle.

'Yeah.' He has reached the swings, sits hunched on the nearest one, his collar up against the cold.

Anna takes the swing next to him. 'It's been years since I've been on one of these.'

They begin to move, pushing off with the tips of their trainers.

Anna tilts her head back and watches the sky rush forward.

They move in time, the seats creaking. There seems no need to speak.

Elliot slows the pace, twizzling the ropes, his swing wound tight. Anna brings her own swing to a juddering stop, just watching. Boris and the collie thunder past the other way.

Elliot's eyes follow them. 'My dad's not that well. He's had a sort of breakdown. After my mum left.'

'I'm sorry.' She wishes she could come up with something better to say. Sorry is bland. Like blank white paper.

'It's a bit hard. Bringing mates home.'

'Of course.' What exactly is a breakdown? Anna doesn't know. She pictures his dad walking very slowly, bumping into things, like a damaged toy robot. 'What does he think about Kris Kowper?'

'My dad's into anything to do with music. Used to play himself once. Almost made it . . .'

'What stopped him?'

Elliot shrugs and doesn't answer. He keeps his eyes on the dogs, and Anna thinks suddenly that she must be poking her sticks into too many secrets. Disturbing too many hidden fish.

'I just . . . wanted to know you better.' This is a risk. Her own fish slipping out and swimming bold and bright with all the sunlight catching its scales.

He shakes his head. Shrugs again. 'Some people reckon I'm not easy to know.'

She gets a rush of feeling when he says this, as if the wind has just blasted through her. She wants to touch him and hold on to him and make everything be all right. But he's too distant. Standing on the other side of the bridge. And she's not certain if he'd want her to cross.

FRIDAY 1 DECEMBER

LIVE AT

THE EDGE

PRESENTS:

SABOTAGE

PLUS SUPPORT ACT **Elliot Heath**

Tickets: £5.00 or £7.50 on the door

DOORS OPEN 8PM

Some tickets remaining!!

Chapter Fifteen

Elliot stares at his reflection in the tinsel-edged mirror. The face that stares back belongs to a stranger, the eyes seeming to search for something. Recognition? Familiarity? Elliot watches the stranger rake his hair. It's the tousled look. Kris reckoned it was sexy. Kris reckoned. Kris reckoned.

The glass is cracked, a long line splitting the middle like a scar. The scar line cuts across the HANDS OFF logo that runs diagonally down his T-shirt.

'Sorry about the mirror.' Geoff Hobbs comes in from the door that leads out to the stage and stands behind him. 'We do get it replaced as often as we can, but it just gets smashed up again.'

'Who by?'

'Bands. They come off stage buzzed up and wired, and start wrecking things. That's why we never go overboard with Christmas decorations.'

Elliot looks round at the shabby dressing room. There are streamers hanging from the ceiling. A scattering of cards. 'Can't you stop them?'

'Me? I'm just the manager. I can't control them. And, really, it's just part of the scene.' Geoff shrugs. 'The best thing for us is if they manage to pull some girls. They can burn their egos out that way then.'

'Not Elliot.' Kris walks in from where he has been checking the fridge for water and fresh fruit, and Elliot and Geoff both turn round. 'He's keeping all his energy for his music.'

Kris comes towards him now and Elliot realizes he has a small pale blue box in his hand. 'Sort of a good luck pressie. I reckon it's just the thing.'

Elliot opens the box. There's a padlock inside, hung on a heavy silver chain. 'What's it for?'

'Final touch. Elliot the Untouchable.' Kris loops it round Elliot's neck. It's heavier than it looks, and Elliot feels the weight of it against his chest. He never wears jewellery.

A ginger-haired sound recorder wearing reindeer antlers on his head pushes in through the dressing room door. 'Two minutes, guys,' he says. He disappears again.

Elliot's hands shake as he lifts his guitar.

'Remember the run-through.' Geoff turns to him. 'You stay by the steps until I introduce you.'

Kris flicks his eyes over Elliot, then stands back for a longer view. 'Remember to make eye contact. The girls will go for that. They'll think you're picking them out.'

Elliot nods but he's hardly listening. He could really blow it tonight. He wishes the college lot weren't going to be out there. He'll have to face them on Monday. Be fed muffins and sympathy. The loser who thought he was going to be something special. And failed.

'You're on,' says Kris. 'Go. Go go go.'

Elliot follows Geoff to the edge of the stage. He can see into the hall. Most of the audience aren't even looking towards the front. They stand in clusters, chatting and drinking. There are more backs than faces. A crush at the bar.

Geoff holds his hands out like a messiah about to reveal that the day of reckoning has come.

And it has.

'We're bringing you another newcomer to The Edge. A newcomer to the whole scene. But it's my view he won't stay new for long. So—put your hands together and let's hear it for the Untouchable Elliot.'

A spotlight burns down on to the centre of the stage. Geoff steps back and Elliot steps forward. Hardly anyone is watching.

Closing his eyes, he feels his way along the guitar strings. There is a hum coming back at him from the audience, people still talking.

'Go for it, Elliot!' The voice from the side gets lost in the drone. Someone else joins in. Then another. 'We love you, Elliot!' 'Go for it!'

He opens his eyes but he can't make out the detail from the huddle at the side of the room. Only that some of the audience are waving and clapping. It must be the college lot. He nods at them. Muffins and sympathy. At least it will make a good lyric. Strumming faster, he moves through the opening chords, and cuts in with 'Trust Thing'. It comes out all wrong, of course. He starts too high. There's feedback from the amp. But at least the crowd grows quiet, even closing in a bit. There are girls resting their elbows on the front of the stage, watching him as if he's whispering secrets to them. As he moves into something faster, a bunch of people begin to dance. By the third number he's starting to relax.

By the next, he's managed the eye contact. Another group of girls start twirling. Glitter in their hair. Tattoos on their bare bellies. More eye contact. He sees a flash of burnt red and Amber elbows past the gyrating tattoos. A small space opens round her—she's that kind of dancer. The kind that people stand back and watch. Then Melissa and Sally and Louise push through, and they're all dancing too.

As he kicks into 'Song for Insomniacs' he risks a smile.

Then he has some fun, giving them an unrehearsed rocked-up version of 'Hark the Herald'. Kris can ball him out for it later if he wants, but everyone's dancing now. And then somehow it's over. Quickly. Too quickly. As he runs back into the dressing room, Kris comes forward with a cold towel. 'Count to twenty,' he says.

'What for?'

'It's important you don't leave it too long.'

'Leave what?'

'They're calling for you. You have to get back out there.'

Elliot lets himself hear, for the first time, the cheers

and the hoots and the thump thump thump of the stamping.

It's not everyone. He's not stupid enough to think the whole room is rocking. But it's enough.

Lead me through the stage door.
Play until my heart's sore.
Sing until my soul's raw.
Want them wanting more.

Chapter Sixteen

Kris waits at the bottom of the steps, ready with iced water.

'They're still calling.' Elliot's eyes are wide and wild, as if he's just been jolted out of a dream. 'What do I do?'

'You let them call this time. Don't give them too much. You have to always leave fans wanting more. Basic psychology. OK?'

'OK.' Elliot peels off the HANDS OFF T-shirt, knocks back half the water, then upturns the bottle and splashes the rest over his face.

'You were good. Listen—and believe it.' Kris's mind is wheeling and reeling. The kid blew everyone away. And he looked great—fantastic. Even with his sweat-drenched hair and T-shirt. Or maybe because of them. They'll need to build on that look more. Maybe get some more pictures done. He'd been hoping a couple of record companies would've made it down tonight, but he hasn't seen anyone. It's disappointing, but he hadn't risked telling Elliot anyway. The kid was tizzed up enough as it was. Maybe they'll show up next time. He'll get on the phone tomorrow. Sabotage are splayed around the dressing room now, messing about, sticking mistletoe everywhere.

Declan Barrett, the sand-blond lead singer who was signed with Kris before he got in with this new band, turns to Elliot. 'That was great.'

The rest of the band pitch in. 'Thanks for the support.'

'Good warm up.'

'Cheers, pal.'

Elliot nods and mumbles something back, collapsing on the one remaining chair. Kris doesn't like seeing him squashed in like that. He wants to see him in a dressing room of his own. Silk and champagne. This kid should have it all. He knows he's trying to move too fast, but it's hard to hold back your imagination when it's shooting out fireworks. And it's been too close for too long. He lost Declan because he didn't tie him in tight enough. He's got a better grip on Elliot. Between the two of them, they're headed for the moon.

'Wanna beer, Elliot?' Declan is already on his third. God knows how these boys are making it. A couple of them already look pretty shot.

'Go for it. Unwind a bit. Now you're finished.' Kris makes it sound as if the decision is his. A reward. It needs to be that way. Elliot needs to listen to him.

He watches Elliot take a can from the bass player, swill it round a bit and have a few sips. He doesn't look as if he's that interested, and that's good. Elliot puts the can down on the floor as his mobile bleeps. Frowning, he checks the text message. Kris frowns too, wondering who it is. The dad? Some girl? He's pushing too hard if he asks, but it's getting to him.

He interrupts Elliot's texted reply. 'Once these boys go on, you ought to go out there and watch. It'll be a good show.'

'It'll be effing brilliant.' Declan laughs, stretching his legs.

Elliot is looking at Declan as if he's some kind of super hero, which isn't good. He doesn't need these guys as role models. 'How's your single doing?'

'Pretty good.' Declan stands up and checks himself in the mirror, combing his hair so that the fringe cuts sideways across his face. 'We're booked to appear on MTV next week.'

Kris feels as if a tiny stick has started drumming inside him. It's the same feeling he used to get when his brother came home with a better school report—or later, with a better looking girlfriend. There was no getting ahead of him. Even his poxy hamster lived longer.

He mustn't take too long getting Elliot moving. There's a mood and a moment, and who knows what competition is pushing its way up through the unknowns. The door opens as the thought begins to jolt through him, not a tiny hammering now, but thundering great thumps. But the feeling stops in mid thud as he spots two familiar faces. 'Hey. Good to see you. I didn't think you'd made it.'

The two men who have walked in shake his hand. The taller one, in a beige suede jacket, claps him on the shoulder. 'We kept at the back. Wanted to stay anonymous.'

Elliot is punching messages into his mobile again.

'Elliot, this is Noel Harrison and . . .' Kris turns, extending his hand to a squat man with a nose like a boxer, 'Tony Hodge.'

'Hi.' Elliot glances at Kris, then at Noel and Tony. He seems distracted and Kris thinks it's good that he doesn't smile. That distant look. He wants these guys to see it's a whole deal. The essence of the kid.

'We're from Obelisk.' Tony's pudged face is grinning, his smile slightly off centre, as if whoever broke his nose shifted his whole face over with the blow. 'Kris sent us the demo and a couple of pics.'

'We wanted to see the action for ourselves.' Noel is the opposite of Tony. Smooth face. Smooth smile.

Kris can see them both looking at Elliot the way he is now—and the way he might turn out.

He wants to chip in that there's not too much work to do, the kid's nearly there. All they've got to do is like him.

'We liked you. You did a good job out there,' says Noel. 'Drew them out.'

Tony laughs. 'And a double encore for a support act was pretty impressive. We liked that too.'

'So . . .' Kris wants to hang on to them. There are so many kids. So many dreams. He wants to burn Elliot into their memory banks, brand them with his brand. 'Have you got some time now? Should we get Elliot showered and go and grab a bite or something?'

'Not now, sorry.' Noel shakes his head. 'We're

headed up north really, and we've got an early start in the morning.'

'This has been a bit of a detour. Flying visit.'

'I know. I know. You're busy guys.' Kris nods and grins. Flatter them. Sound grateful.

'Noel and me need to talk some of this through.' Tony is still smiling.

What's the psychology here? Smiling must be good. Promising.

'And we'll be in touch,' adds Noel. 'Some time after Christmas.'

'Sure.' Kris keeps his grin going. Being in touch is promising too. They've turned up. They've come backstage. They're going to talk, and Christmas isn't far away. He can't ask much more for now. Top guys like these aren't going to give anything away too soon.

They know better than that.

Basic psychology.

Chapter Seventeen

The wooden floor is sticky with beer. 'Like a frigging ice rink,' grins the bouncer. His muscles bulge through a tight black vest as he stands, arms folded, outside the dressing room door.

'Yeah.' Elliot steps past him, feeling awkward now that he's out amongst the throng. The room throbs with a disco beat, a mix of dancers and shouters and laughers and talkers and everyone seems to be part of it except him. The air is fogged in a thin veil of smoke.

He sees the tattoo girls and their eyes, close up, are hardened with dark lines of make-up. Not that they're looking at him. They've pinned down a couple of blokes—more tattoos—and they're all checking each other over and talking too fast and one of the blokes has his hand on the tallest girl's backside.

Elliot heads towards the bar. Some people glance or edge sideways to let him elbow past, but he could be anyone. The beer is too warm and too bitter and it slops when he walks, people knocking into him and not even stopping or glancing round as he heads for some space at the back of the hall. And he wants suddenly to be out of all this. It was just a sham, up there on the stage. A fantastic moment, but emptied of anything real.

'ELLIOT!!' Sally and Melissa rush at him, grabbing his arm and pulling him round. Their words are thin snatches struggling against the hub and thrum of the disco.

'. . . fantastic . . .'

'Hey . . .'

'Rory says . . .'

'. . . next?' Sally hugs him and his beer slushes down on to the floor again. Melissa tweaks the silver 'final touch' padlock.

'Great stuff.' Rory strides over, claps his shoulder, then looks round the room. 'You seen Amber?'

'No.'

'She's disappeared. I've tried . . .' He says something that Elliot can't catch, still scanning faces as he talks. Elliot knows what Rory's going through. Knows what Amber's like. He wants to tell him she isn't worth it, but he's not likely to listen. He wouldn't have listened either, at the time.

There is a louder burr of voices as the disco fades away, and Geoff steps back on to the stage.

'And now—thank you for your patience—let's hear a wild roar of welcome for SABOTAGE!'

The band burst out like firecrackers, the music snapping the air. Elliot thinks they look bigger somehow—not just higher up, but physically bigger. All around him everyone is bouncing and jumping and waving their arms. A girl in a plunging red top skids and slides into him. He loses the second third of his beer.

But the music is kicking in, like a drug topping him back up, and by the end of the first number he's in the moment again. Thinking about his own songs. There are things he could change. He could bring in a faster sound next time, blast out at the audience right from the start. He ought to get home and write. Write. Write. He's got to get this down before it flies away. Ideas are like dreams. You give them some space and they get lost in it. And once they're gone, they never come back. 'I'm wrecked,' he mouths to Sally. 'I've got to go.'

'Great, aren't they,' she shouts back, grabbing his hands and trying to force him to dance.

He twists away. Finding a ledge to leave what's left of his beer on, he heads back to get his bag. The dressing room is full of strangers now. Loved-up girls and blokes and all of them with SABOTAGE across their T-shirts.

Someone has sprayed 'I Love you Declan' all over the mirror in fake snow. At least it isn't smashed up. Yet.

They all turn to look at Elliott.

'I saw you.' A girl with grunge hair lurches over to him. She is chewing gum and her eyes are very bright. 'I liked you.'

'Thanks.' Elliot stands awkwardly. They are all still staring. 'Just came back to grab my things.'

'You can grab mine if you like,' another girl calls from over on the couch.

Laughter bubbles up slowly, as if it takes a while for everyone to work out what she said.

Elliot edges past them, pushing open the door to the shower, and knocking a clump of mistletoe that slides slowly down on to the cracked tile floor. His bag is in there. He'll just grab it, and go. He's not comfortable with this lot.

'Don't go in . . .' drawls a tall bloke with a peppered grey ponytail.

But it's too late. Elliot is already there. He doesn't look for long, but it's long enough. Long enough to see Amber's moon-pale limbs wrapped around some guy with a tattoo on his naked back. Neither of them even look up.

Elliot grabs his bag and turns away.

'Sorry.' Peppered ponytail grins at him. 'Tried to warn you.'

'It's OK.' Elliot shrugs. 'Don't think it was a problem for them.'

As he heads back out to find Kris, he's thinking that he's not going to say anything to Rory. Rory will have to find out the hard way, just like he did. Amber. Bad news. Are all girls like that, deep down? And just as he thinks this, his mobile goes again. Anna. They've been texting a lot. He's been getting to like her. But maybe he should hold back. He's got songs to write. It would be crazy to risk messing himself up with a girl again.

Gotta get out
before the trouble starts.
Before the guns of need
blast both our hearts.

A STORMING NIGHT OUT

The sell-out gig featuring Sabotage hit like a tidal wave at The Edge last night. Declan Barrett, the lead singer, ebbed and flowed with a range of hits from 'Swing Me High' to the surf crashing sound of 'Terminal Tantrum'.

The venue also turned the tide with a debut performance by new face Elliot Heath, who washed in with a storming fresh sound, and got the audience frothing for more — unusual in an unknown supporting act.

'We like to encourage new talent, and Elliot proved last night that his is definitely a name to watch for,' enthused Edge Manager Geoff Brooks.

Jim Lambert

For a comprehensive list of coming entertainment, make sure you order your copy of What's On — out every Friday.

Chapter Eighteen

'I wish I'd been there.' Anna is cross-legged on her bed, her brush blurring a line round the water-colour portrait of his face. 'Mum was a pain. Saying I was too young.'

Elliot switches the CD over to Traci Maran, and wonders how long it took Anna to paint silver stars on her toenails.

He hadn't meant to come. And it's his own fault. Last night, stuck on a lyric about the sham that was Christmas and staring out of his bedroom window at the rain, he'd felt a grey weight press down on him. So he'd sent her a text. It was only a short one, but she'd flashed an answer straight back and then later she'd rung him.

After they'd talked the song came out OK and the grey weighted feeling had gone. That was why he came.

Anna holds the paper up to the light, moving it at different angles. 'What d'you think?'

'Yeah. It's good.' She's caught him—not so much the likeness, but the feel of him. As if she's managed to get under the skin.

He thinks, as he looks at it, that it is that under the skin bit that makes it good. Any art. Words and music and paintings and poems. There's no point reproducing the surface. The surface is already there.

He looks up at her and she's looking at him. 'You OK?'

'Yeah. Thanks.'

He gets the feeling she probably isn't and he remembers the last time they got together, when she was asking a hundred and one questions about his dad. *'I want to know you better,'* she'd said. And she'd flushed after she'd said it and bitten her lip as if she wished she'd held the words in. It's always too late, once you've let the words out. They dance about on their own. They change shape in people's minds. They cause arguments. Wars. It's one of the reasons he sticks with lyrics. Words are controlled when they're caught in a song. He can make them big or small or angry or painful and they still only stay in the places he's put them.

'I want to know you better.'

It's just an impulse and he doesn't quite know why but he reaches for her hand and she lets him take it. Their fingers press into each other as if they are talking through touch. 'Come to the next gig. I'll get you on the guest list—you and a mate.' He thinks at least he can do that. 'I'll talk to your mum. If you want.'

'I want.'

They both stare down at their fingers, still tightly laced. Is this about gigs? He doesn't know.

Traci Maran comes to an end.

The CD clicks off.

Silence hangs.

He's not sure next whether he leans towards her, or if she leans towards him. But suddenly he is gripping her arm and she has reached for his other hand and they are so fumbly and so clumsy and it would look to anyone watching like the first kiss in the world ever. And, in a way, it is.

When it is finished she draws away slowly. 'You'll forget me, once you're famous.'

He looks at her. She smells like vanilla. There are gold flecks in her eyes. 'Why?'

'Because you'll be able to get anyone. Any girl you want.'

He shifts beside her, drifting on what's going through him. Not the heat and lust that drove him mad with Amber. This is softening. A watercolour moment.

'I don't want any girl. Only one.'

When he says this she seems to sigh as if there is something she has been holding in, then rests her head against him and the afternoon slides into evening and words are not part of anything that matters.

Just tryin' to find
a way to say,
you take the grey
away.

Chapter Nineteen

Mary watches Elliot sprawl across the sofa. She ought to tell him to take his trainers off—they'll mark the new beige covers—but she knows it will just cause more tension, and she doesn't want that. Not on Christmas Day. There's too much wrong between them as it is.

'That was good. Great entertainment.' Sheldon turns to her as the Comedy Classic Christmas Special ends. 'What do you want next?'

'We could play a game.' She is hating her voice as she says it. Bright and hopeful and all on the surface. 'I think I've got Scrabble upstairs . . .'

'Not for me.' Elliot glances at his watch. 'I need to get off soon. I'm meeting someone.'

'A girl?' Mary can't help herself. She does this all the time, scratching at the closed door of his life, trying to find a way in.

Elliot doesn't answer. He just sits up straighter, leaning forward slightly, drumming his fingers against his leg. At least she doesn't have to feel anxious about his trainers on the beige covers any more.

Mary wants to drop her head in her hands and cry.

Most of the time, in her new safe Sheldon life,

she's happy. Day to day, she's happy. But every now and then, the pain of everything that's wrong knocks her sideways.

'I feel like a lump.' Sheldon stands up, stretches, then comes over and touches her hair. 'We should've done a run after dinner.'

Mary sees Elliot glance at the gesture, and drum faster.

'Not me,' she says quickly, tilting her head away. 'It is Christmas, after all. We need to relax a bit.' That bright ridiculous voice again. She throws a smile at Elliot, desperate to bring him in. Keep him talking. 'What did you and Dad have to eat?'

His dark eyes meet hers. Bottomless. Unfathomable. 'Sausage and chips.'

'Oh.' A silly squeak of a sound. Mary knows that if she watched herself—saw herself as a character in a play, for instance—she'd find herself so irritating. And she knows that's how Elliot sees her. Irritating, and worse.

'We did a roast. OK?' Elliot is suddenly aggressive. His voice dark. 'We *do* still celebrate, you know.'

'I'm sorry, I . . .'

'Now, now,' says Sheldon, nodding round at them both, 'how about we . . .'

'No—not for me.' Elliot gets up, going over to the small stack of jumpers and smellies and HMV vouchers that are under the tree.

Mary knows he despises the tree—despises it for being artificial—but Sheldon brought it back from

B&Q about four years ago, excited that they wouldn't have to suffer pine needles any more.

So different to Billy. Billy used to drive out to the forest and dig one up, every Christmas Eve. There were pine needles everywhere by New Year's Day. She was always vacuuming them up. 'But it's the smell of them,' Billy had always insisted. 'Don't you think the smell of them is beautiful?'

'I'm going.' Elliot pushes all his presents into one carrier bag, and nods round at her.

'I'll see you to the door.' Mary stands and walks with him into the hallway. Following behind him she thinks how tall he's getting. She flashes up a memory of herself holding him, a tiny baby, in the maternity home where she'd stayed after she left the hospital. Elliot must have been about two days old. Billy had been in earlier, but it had been a rushed visit because he had a rehearsal. After he left she sat by the old sash window, looking out at the late summer garden, thinking she at last understood what happiness was. She held Elliot close then, loving him so much, his tiny warmth snuggled against her. And he smelt beautiful.

At the door now he turns to her awkwardly. 'Bye then, Mum. Happy Christmas.'

She leans forward, going for a clumsy hug. He stoops down to let her kiss the side of his face, but he doesn't touch her.

She thinks, as she watches him walk away from her through the foggy night, that he still smells beautiful.

Chapter Twenty

'What is it you want from your music career?' Steve Dodds has steel-grey hair and rimless glasses. Elliot thinks he looks too normal to be the director of a mega music label. But then they all look normal. Eleven men in dark jackets or suits. A woman in a pink dress. This circle of people who can weave dreams. Change lives. You could pass them in the street and have no idea.

He squints across at the pictures on the wall opposite, looking for his answer among the gallery of stars. Was every one of those stars here, like this? Sitting round this heavy oak table? A full length shot of a bloke with a guitar startles him and makes him lean forward, thinking it's someone he knows. And then it hits him that it's Marc Wild. He looks young. Younger than Elliot. And raw.

'I want to last.' He keeps his eyes on the raw, young Marc. 'I want to be good now, and good in twenty years.'

He gets the feeling that Marc is looking back at him. On his side.

Steve Dodds's voice nudges him. 'Just good?'

Elliot shifts a look at him then. Of course not just good. Brilliant. Amazing. To lift people. To move people. His mind runs back to a time when he was around seven. Maybe eight at the most. He was in the back of the old blue Datsun, out on one of the dreaded family outings that always ended with Mum and Dad storming at each other, and Dad drowning her out with a blare from the car radio.

Elliot remembers he was sucking a peppermint for carsickness, rolling it round the inside of his mouth and staring out at a mass of dark clouds that were already spitting down on to the window. The rain was cold and hard. The world was cold and hard. And then Marc came on the radio. The title track from an album called 'Driving Seat'—all all about a bloke who was taking control of his life. It was the first time Elliot properly understood about lyrics and meanings, and it was like lights coming on. The music filled the car. He couldn't hear Mum and Dad any more and he didn't feel sick.

He pulls himself back into the present. 'I want . . .' He says the words slowly, rolling them like a peppermint in his mouth, 'to make people know there's always something more. Whatever crap is going on, they can blot it out and get lifted by music. I want to be as good as that.'

He looks away quickly, but Steve Dodds is smiling and so are all the dream weavers, and it's as if he's said some fantastic, incredible thing that is going to change the world. 'We're going for a three single deal, and we'll be releasing an album in the spring. You've all heard the first single, and I've no doubt

Elliot will pull through with two new ones that are just as hot,' he says.

Noel Harrison nods round at the others. '"Untouchable" gets released four months from today. It'll be—let's see—' He glances at Tony Hodge, who does a scribbled calculation on a pad of paper.

'18 April,' says Tony.

'That's a Monday,' Noel explains. 'Singles are always released on a Monday.'

'In the meantime,' Steve Dodds puts his hands behind his head and leans back, 'we need to get to work on the video. We'll organize all that through Kris. Get a few treatments—' he flicks another smile at Elliott, '—that's ideas and scripts—from some of the top people, then organize the shoot once they've come up with something that works.'

The pink-dress woman smiles. 'Six weeks before the release we get you out there properly. We get you radio airplay. Interviews in all the right places. We'll be pushing the "Untouchable" image. That's vital for the brand.'

'And then,' Noel's smile is dazzling, 'we watch you move up the chart.'

'All the way.' Kris is dazzling too, speaking for the first time.

'All the way.' The dream weavers are all dazzling. The whole room dazzling. Maybe the whole world.

Elliot can feel his dreams moving, changing colour, curling and drifting and washing through him. This is more than his dream. It's his life. The bones of him. Make it all happen. Make it all work. *Please. Please.*

'There's just one other thing.' Steve Dodds stretches his hands out flat on the table. 'It's been added to the contract, and it's something we talked over with Kris before you got here.'

Elliot is up for anything. He'll shave his head. Paint himself green. Dance through the streets in a pink spangled tutu. 'What?'

'Girlfriends,' says Steve.

'What?'

'The deal is that you don't have any. Not while we're building the brand.'

Elliot stares down at his own hands, thinking about Anna. He's feeling sick; a kid who's eaten too many peppermints. The pink spangled tutu would have been better than this.

Tony scratches the end of his nose. 'It doesn't work anyway. Girls seem up for it at first, but after a while they get tired of you being away so much.'

Kris is nodding his agreement: 'It's a lot of pressure on girlfriends, just sitting at home waiting and wondering what you're up to.'

Elliot studies the patterns on the table, the dark grain worn into the rich, solid oak. How will he tell her? How can he tell her? She painted a picture of him playing on stage for his Christmas present—she did it in secret, from a photo that was in the *Newton News,* and gave it to him in a hand decorated frame. In the taxi that brought him here, she sent a hundred texts. She rang before he left. She is the last thing he thinks of before he goes to sleep.

Steve Dodds hands the contract across the table.

Noel brings him a gold pen on a blue silk cushion. 'Company policy,' he says. 'It's only used for signing.'

The dream weavers are all smiling.

In the front of the old blue Datsun, Mum spat words at Dad like cold rain. Dad gave up his dreams, and a drowning relationship was what he woke up to. The young, raw Marc Wild sat at this very table.

Elliot picks up the pen. As he signs, his signature swirls out in a shape he doesn't recognize.

The door opens and a girl swishes in, champagne and glasses on a gold oval tray. The pink-dress woman stands and shakes the bottle. The cork pops, a froth of bubbling silver fizzing down on to the grained table.

Everyone has a glass to raise. 'To Elliot,' they say. 'To Elliot.'

Sold my name
the day it rained
champagne.

Music & Blues

The One to Watch

Obelisk Records have started the New Year by announcing a new signing — Elliot Heath, from Westhill.

'Elliot has blown us away,' says Steve Dodds, Obelisk's director. 'I don't want to load this boy with too much pressure, but we're pretty excited about this discovery. His style is dynamite. Think Marc Wild, with maybe a bit of Bobby Lewis peppered in. But alongside the voice and the sound he's got a look that is startling. That mix of talent and stark good looks makes him star material. This is a boy who could go straight to the top.'

Charlotte Mayhew

Chapter Twenty-One

Schedule for today: 10.15 newspaper interview
Midday—lunch Kris and Pete K (Obelisk)
2p.m. photos (@ WP Station)
3p.m. newspaper interview.
4p.m. sound check Liberty Hall
8p.m. gig (remember spare strings/plectrums)

'You can't do all this. It's ridiculous.'

Elliot turns back from the window at the sound of Mum's voice, his mind still tangled with the lyrics he's just been trying out. He wanted to bring the dawn in—to use it as a metaphor for the cruelty of a new beginning. Blood orange. He still hasn't told Anna.

'Elliot—I said it's ridiculous.'

'What?'

She picks up his notepad from the kitchen table and waves it at him. 'This schedule.'

'That's private.' He takes the pad back from her, shoves it into his jacket pocket.

Mum fusses with the belt on her silk dressing gown and shakes her head. 'I wanted to check everything was all right. You never tell me anything. We hardly ever see you.'

Elliot feels a tightening in his head. He only slipped away from home because his head was buzzing and he couldn't sleep, but Dad was already prowling downstairs and he couldn't face the hundred and one 'How's it all going, son?' questions. He can't face this outburst from Mum either. 'Everything's fine.'

'Well, I don't *know* that, do I? All I know about you is what I read in newspapers, or what friends ring me up and tell me.'

'It's going OK.'

'OK?' Her eyes have a watery film over them now. 'You're being whisked away from normality, and I want to try and slow you down.'

He looks back out into the garden. She doesn't want to slow him down. She wants to grind him to a halt. Put the lid on him.

'You've got to keep a steady head. Keep your course going. Get your degree. Fame doesn't always last. You don't want to end up like . . .' She grinds to a halt. Puts the lid on what she was going to say.

Elliot turns back to the window.

It is going to be cold, the sky stretched and pale, like the skin on a drum. A blackbird hops noisily along the edge of the fence. In the far corner, underneath a straggling bush, a sparrow is scratching for food. It's true, Elliot thinks, about things being OK. The schedule's tight, but it doesn't wear him out. And he can't stop writing. Since that time with Anna he can't stop new ideas for songs from growing. More and more ideas keep spreading through him. It's as if hundreds of songs have been waiting, curled up inside him, and now they're being allowed to unfurl.

Upstairs, in the bathroom, the pipes creak as the shower turns off. Sheldon will be down soon. Elliot turns away from the window again. 'I need to go,' he says. 'I've got a car coming to get me from Westhill Road at nine.'

'Just—think about what I say. I mean it for the best. If you'd only . . .'

Elliot's mobile goes off, a number he doesn't recognize. 'Hello?'

'Elliot? I'm Josh Steine. We met at Obelisk last week.'

'Hi. Were you the promotions guy?'

'That's it—the plugger—and I need to check a few dates with you. Once the single's out I'm going to need complete availability for the next three weeks at least. Are you OK with that?'

'Yeah, sure. I can do whenever.'

Behind him Mum sighs, then pads away upstairs.

'I need to get you up here just before the actual release so I can run through what direction we're taking with all the promos. I always keep artists completely up to date with what's going on, and I know you're still studying, so we might have to juggle times a bit.'

Elliot pushes the kitchen door and walks into the garden. 'No, it's OK. I'll fit with you.'

'That's great. We need to get as much airplay as possible. Someone will be in touch about the video shoot. And I'm organizing a mass of those T-shirts for when you start touring properly. They'll shift well at gigs.'

'Great.'

'So—any worries?'

Elliot was right. It *is* cold out. But he likes the bite of it. The sense of clarity it gives. He watches a dusk-grey cat stalk through rags of nettles, creeping like a shadow behind the wire fence at the back. The black-bird shouts noisily. The sparrow flutters up, spinning away.

'Elliot? You still there?'

'Yeah. Sorry. No. No worries.'

'Great—well, give me a call if you think of anything. And fingers crossed, although I don't reckon you'll need it. I've got a hunch about you, and I'm good at instincts.'

Elliot walks back into the kitchen and through to the hall. Mum appears, dressed now. Sheldon is behind her, his hair ruffed up and wet, a towel round his waist. 'I'm sorry if I'm going on at you,' says Mum.

'You should listen to her.' Sheldon puts his hands on her shoulders, his fingers kneading the fabric of her blouse. 'She's on your side. She just doesn't want you to throw your future away.'

Elliot looks at them both and he doesn't know them. He could pass them in the street. The plugger feels more real to him than them.

'You're right.' Elliot pushes his hand into his pocket

and feels the edge of the notebook. He doesn't want to throw his future away either. They can't have two people in the family messing up like that.

Let strangers
rearrange tomorrow.
Cut the cord.
The leaking sunrise
bleeds its sorrow.

Chapter Twenty-Two

Kris presses the 'send' button and pours himself a drink to celebrate. The whole Elliot machine is purring along. He's just emailed Obelisk and attached a bio for the website, and he's already setting up venues for the spring tour.

They'll have to work twenty-four seven, but the kid's hungry enough to want to push it all through. That's the main thing. Staying hungry. And he doesn't see Elliot as the type of kid who'd be daft enough to push the plate away.

Chapter Twenty-Three

It's getting dark. A brittle evening. The taxi stitches slowly along, all the traffic knotting up at the round-about near her road. They're late, and Elliot's glad. It gives him more time to run the moment through his head. More time to find a way to say it right.

He's just come back from London—bunking off college for a lunchtime studio rehearsal with Kris and some guys who are going to do the backing. He's knackered, but there's a stack of stuff to get through—especially now they've confirmed the tour dates. He's got to get himself sorted—organize his time and stick his head in it.

And then there's Anna.

He's been avoiding her all week, and now he's got to get it over with. He pictures himself doing it as soon as he sees her, a gabbled apology the minute she appears. Maybe she'll shove him away, storm back into her house. It'll be over, and he won't be leading her on any more. He'll have done the right thing.

'This it?' The driver turns his head to look at him.

Elliot wants to tell him to drive on. Pull away with a screech of brakes like someone in a car chase. Coward. 'Yeah. This is it. You can pull in by the bus stop.'

Anna comes running out of her front door, as if

she's been watching for him. Elliot doesn't want that. Doesn't want her to have been watching.

'I've been watching for you,' she says. She links her arm through his, steering him towards the gate, but he holds back.

'Can we walk into town? Go for coffee or something?' He needs to be somewhere neutral. He can't do this in the friendly clutter of her room.

'Anywhere. I just want to hear every detail.' She's wearing that jacket again, the one with wild roses, but this time she has her hair pinned up, rebel strands straying across her face. 'We'll try Fat Tuesdays. They do a great cappuccino—it's not far.'

It strikes him that she looks different every time he sees her. But always beautiful.

They pass the newsagent on the corner, the local *Newton News* headline shouting a protest about 'Bus Lane Blunder'. Kris has told Elliot he's getting another mention in there soon. In loads of local papers. Obelisk is sending out a press release.

'I've been making candles. They're part of my art project at school for this new term. I'll show them to you when you come back later.' Anna's chatter blows cold breath into the night.

Elliot thinks suddenly that it's better to never get involved with people. Never to soften and melt against them. Girls. Mates. Parents. It all ends up a waxy mess in the end.

She takes his hand and he lets her keep it, her fingers lacing with his. Her grip is warm and firm.

The grip of someone who is where they want to be. He'll always remember her. She'll always be someone who mattered.

A woman steers a buggy at them, the baby inside red-faced and screaming, fists punching the air. They drop hands, Elliot stepping into the gutter to let the buggy through. A car blasts its horn at him. Elliot waves an apology. Back on the pavement, Anna's hand finds his again.

Up ahead he can see the lights of Fat Tuesdays. The neon green sign. A steaming white mug painted on the outside of the window.

Inside there is jazz music playing. It patterns the background, lifting the late night shoppers burdened with bargains from the January sales. He picks up a tray and edges along the counter, Anna pressed against him. He can smell her hair. Vanilla. How is he going to tell her? How is he going to start? He pays at the till in a trance, almost forgetting his change. Anna leads him to a table at the back of the cafe.

'We'll sit here. Where it's quiet.' She wriggles out of her jacket, draping it over the back of the chair. It still looks like her, even hanging empty. If you had to pick jackets for anyone in the café, you'd pick the wild roses velvet for her. Her look. Her brand. Not everyone has that about them. He wonders if anyone would pick out the Hands Off T-shirts for him. He keeps his own jacket on. He might not be staying long.

'So . . .' She tilts her head on one side. 'Tell me

now. Every intricate wonderful fantastic detail.'

He empties a sachet of brown sugar into the froth of his coffee, watching it melt slowly before it sinks away. 'I dunno. Sometimes things aren't exactly what you think.'

'It didn't go wrong, did it? They did sign you properly and everything?' Her eyes are troubled as she looks across at him. 'I kept thinking and thinking about how it was all going. I know it sounds stupid, but I felt so helpless, and in the end I lit a candle for you. A sort of prayer.'

Something flashes up in him. A thin flame of anger. He hadn't asked her for candles and prayers. He doesn't even believe in crap like that. His voice when he speaks is stiff and gruff and he's glad of the change of mood. 'You think prayers work?'

She gives a small shake of her head. 'I don't know. I hope so.'

'Well, if they do, you should have better things to pray for. There's kids starving in Africa.'

She frowns, then stares down at a spill of sugar on the table, tracing it with her finger. 'I know. It must sound empty and shallow and stupid. But it's just that you—out of all the people I've ever met or seen or known—have got something special. If you don't make it, then nobody should.'

He's hardly listening. 'Even in this country there's people with all sorts of rubbish going on. Homeless. Hungry.' Elliot grips this idea like a beggar with a bowl. 'Save the prayers for them.'

The jazz backing blasts them with a blare of solo saxophone.

'I've upset you.' Her eyes smoke over. 'But maybe, even in what you've just said, there's a deeper meaning.'

'Like what?' Maybe if he keeps flicking hot embers at her she'll just get up and walk away. That would be easier. Coward. Coward.

'I believe in fate—that everything happens for a reason. If things like starving people matter to you, then maybe you'll do something special with the fame. Charity gigs. Hospital visits. You know.' Her eyes find his again. 'If you look for good, you'll find it—and maybe that's why you've got the talent in the first place—because you'll use it properly. You won't just take and take.'

He stares back at her and the anger burns out. He's thought of that himself. Getting rich isn't what's driving him forward. He wants the name, and the fame, but not for the money. He's not in it for that. He feels suddenly as if he's seeing her for the first time. She's amazing. And she lit a candle for him. He's not sure that anyone's ever done that before. Not done something just for him, without wanting anything back.

'I'm sorry. I'm in a weird mood.'

She reaches across the table, takes his hand. He holds on to her, his grip warm and firm. Someone who is where they want to be.

'I bet it was brilliant up at Obelisk,' she says. 'All this hedging is just because you're too modest.'

The smile she blows him is flame bright. She is

velvet and wild roses. He doesn't need to tell her everything yet. 'You're right.' He nods. 'Obelisk was good. I'll tell you about it, but just don't tell your mates or anyone.'

'Why?'

'Just . . .' He hesitates. 'Everything has to be kept quiet for a while. Kris wants it like that. You and me too . . . it's all a bit complicated. Just needs to be handled properly.'

'OK. If that's what we have to do.'

'Not for ever. Just . . .' He stops again. It still sounds bad. It still sounds as if he's asking too much.

'Stop worrying.' Her fingers lace his again. 'I'm on your side. I've been there right from the beginning. Just tell me how it went. Please.'

'OK.' He feels himself grinning suddenly. A bubbled excitement fills him. She's been there from the beginning—how could he *not* tell her how it went. 'There were twelve of them, and . . .'

Later, when he walks her back home, he lets himself kiss her again.

It doesn't feel like he's doing the wrong thing. It doesn't feel wrong at all.

She lit her lovely candles
at the altar of my mind.
Heard some bloke say,
'It's all OK—
Just seek and you will find.'

HMV – WESTHILL

* Signing by Local Artist *

Elliot

Get a copy of

'Untouchable'

Tour tickets,
T-shirts —
all available
in store

FROM 10A.M.
THIS SATURDAY

Chapter Twenty-Four

Elliot is sitting on the sofa, his eyes skimming the morning paper he isn't even trying to read. Dad fusses with the deck, checking that everything is OK. The newscaster's voice booms in too loud, and too crackling. *'Good morning. And here is the Six O'Clock News.'*

'Damn, I can't get the balance of sound right.' Dad rubs one ear, and then the other. Shakes his head as if he is trying to get something out.

'Kris will get a copy.' Elliot says this without looking up. 'You don't need to record it.'

'I want my own. It's a big moment. I don't want to take any chances. Sssssh. Listen now. It's starting.'

Elliot keeps on looking at the paper, but he *is* listening. The truth is, he's been awake all night, waiting for the moment when he can start to listen.

'Hi, there. This is Danny Gorman. Warming your morning with the newest sounds of today.'

'That's you.' Dad's head makes small pecking movements. 'Sounds of today.'

Elliot folds the paper, then lets it drop to the carpet. 'It could be ages yet. It's a two hour show. Josh Steine couldn't pin down the time it would come on.' He says 'it' rather than 'I'.

'No matter.' Dad fumbles for a chair and pulls it up close to the radio. 'We'll just be rooted here until it does.'

'And first, kicking off with her new hit that's storming up the charts—Traci Maran and "Lilac Ladies" . . .'

Elliot stands abruptly. 'I'll make tea,' he mutters. 'Call me in if . . . you know . . .'

Out in the kitchen he rubs the flat of his hand on the window, looking out at the misted garden. He can see smudged lights in the huddled houses over the back. Are they listening to Danny Gorman too? He pours the tea and carries it back through to the front room.

'Nothing's happened.' Dad is staring at the radio as if it might be tricking him in some way. He flicks fluff off his dressing gown sleeve. 'Maybe it's playing your song beneath the jingles?'

'It's OK, Dad.' Elliot sighs. Maybe they've switched it to a different station without telling anyone. Maybe aliens are somehow beaming the song away on to another planet. 'Honestly. It's OK.' He drops down on to the sofa again. His eyes sting, as if they've got sand in them, and he knows it's because he was working too late, trying to juggle a college assignment with putting a new song together. The new song was the ball that stayed in the air. 'Light Me A Candle'. It isn't quite finished but it's getting there. It's got a strong riff and a great beginning. Kris reckons good songs have an ideal form—a three or four minute verse, then a chorus, then another verse—so he's exploring that format. Elliot doesn't always agree with him, but he's got to try and learn from Kris.

The assignment is still on the floor at the bottom of his bed. He could take a look at it now, but even the idea of the journey upstairs to get it feels huge. All his study work feels like that now. Slow and ugly. Slugs in his head. The songs are yellow butterflies.

'And later on this morning we've got an interview with Declan Barrett of Sabotage, recently back from a sell-out tour in Scotland. And we're giving away free—that's right, free—CDs in our Buzz Rite Breakfast Quiz.'

'Rubbish. It's all rubbish.' Dad has slid down from his chair and is crouched by the radio now, rocking slightly. 'Why doesn't he just get on with the music?'

Elliot wonders suddenly if it's a good thing to be listening. He'll tune into all the faults. Shouldn't he just get on with the new stuff? Do writers ever read their own books once they're finished?

'And next up, one of my favourites in the charts at the moment—"Crazy Cookie" by The Sessions.'

'I'll do some toast.' Elliot knocks back his tea and gets up again.

'Not hungry.' Dad rubs his ear. 'Too nervous.'

'For God's sake, Dad.' He goes back into the kitchen, dropping the bread into the toaster. The smell of burning wafts out. Old crumbs. He ought to clean it soon. Or buy a new one. And when that one starts smelling, he'll buy another new one. New toasters. New cookers. New kitchens. If only he could buy Dad a new life.

Out in the garden the mist has lifted. A pigeon calls from the back fence. The trees are in bud now, tiny lime tips on the branches, the colours all shifting with the lightening day. Kris is sending a car at nine, and he's doing a local HMV signing at ten. They've got some pre-release demos, and a stack of posters to give away. It's the first time they've done anything public like that, and Elliot's not sure anyone will turn up, but Kris has run an ad for it in the *Westhill Weekly*, and there're a mass of flyers stuck all over town. 'We'll pull in local support first,' Kris said. 'And then move up from there.'

Elliot's supposed to be at college this morning, but he's hoping to make it back some time in the afternoon. That's what he's told the tutor anyway. Sometimes Kris has other ideas.

Back in the front room he crunches on the toast, pulling open the curtains to look out at the road. There are a couple of girls hanging around out there, and as soon as they see him they start waving. He raises his toast to them, and closes the curtains again. He doesn't recognize them, but they must be local. Westhill Estate isn't a place you'd visit to admire the scenery. *'And next—someone we don't hear enough from any more—the title track from his last album "Lost and Still Looking"—Marc Wild . . .'*

'Come on, come on.' Dad voice is stretched and urgent, like a gambler watching horses race towards the finish.

'You know when you were getting started . . . ?'

Elliot says this almost without thinking. It's as if the thought in his head has come alive and burrowed its way out.

Dad picks at his sleeve. 'What about it?'

'Can we talk about it?'

The room grows an odd stillness. Everything holding its breath. But, Dad *ought* to talk about it. Even if it all melted and warped and went out of tune, he had moments like this. A bit of time to shine. Or is that what makes it too hard? Is it worse to get so close, and then to have it all scratched away?

What you don't know about, you don't want.

Mum used to say that.

Maybe Mum was right sometimes.

Dad looks up at Elliot, then away, then up again. He plucks harder at his sleeve. Really rubs at it. Elliot can't bear to watch him, and looks down at the crumbs on his plate, wondering if there's a lyric there. The crumbs of the past. Too obvious, too cliched, but he can work on it.

'If I could somehow go back to the beginning again . . .' Dad speaks so softly, Elliot almost doesn't hear, and when he does hear it's suddenly too late, because the 'Still Looking' Marc Wild fades, blending and then disappearing behind a sound that is as much a part of Elliot as his hands. Or his heart. 'Untouchable'.

As the sound threads the room Elliot imagines the world outside. This song—his song—is weaving through rooms all across the country. People are listening at breakfast tables. Getting snatches of it as they run around cursing and searching for their keys. They have it on in cars. On headphones. On radios next to their beds. What are they thinking? What are they saying? Are they taking any notice of it at all?

'. . . And that is a sound I'm sure we'll be hearing a lot more of over the next few weeks. It's blown me away. Blown us all away in the studio here. "Untouchable", by a newcomer to the scene—a young guy known as Elliot . . .'

Elliot looks up slowly. Dad is grinning, almost sparkling, tears streaming down his face. The phone rings. As Elliot heads to the hall to pick it up he hears someone shouting in the street. Opening the front door he glances out, thinking it might be a fight, or someone in trouble. And for a moment he can't take it in. There is a line of girls pressed along the front wall and crushed together by the gate. When they see him they start to scream, their arms stretched out, the front ones running up the drive towards him.

'Elliot! Elliot! Elliot!'

He lurches backwards, slamming the door behind him. They are pressing against the glass. Fingers search through the letterbox.

'Elliot! Elliot! Elliot!'

'What's happening?' Dad is behind him, his eyes boggling, as if the fingers are about to be followed by a whole arm, and then a full body sliding through. Girls being posted into their hallway. 'This is danger. Bad, bad danger. Quickly, quickly. We've got to find somewhere to hide.'

That's my song in your kitchen.
Did you hear the Morning Man mention my name?
That's my song in your kitchen.
Turn it up
and listen
please
again.

Chapter Twenty-Five

Elliot stands in front of the gilt-edged mirror, the Lyric's white monogrammed towel soft round his waist. He's wondering about his chest. Kris reckons he should work out, pump a bit of iron and build himself up. 'Girls go for that,' he said. But girls are going for him anyway. He's been getting knickers in the post. He fingers the padlock that always hangs round his neck, then presses it hard into his skin. There is a moment when the silver bites cold, but almost immediately the sensation is gone. Elliot thinks it's amazing how quickly uncomfortable things can start to feel OK.

He hears the clicking of heels from outside, and a knock on the dressing room door. 'Yeah?' He thinks it must be Sophie, come to do his make-up. He's got used to make-up too. Almost.

There's a pause, and he guesses she's probably struggling with all her bags and boxes as usual, and he's about to go and give her a hand when the door opens. The woman teetering there on dangerously high heels is probably in her early twenties. 'Paige Melder. Here for the interview.'

'I'm not booked for interviews.' He glances past her at the schedule which is pinned on the wall above the clothes rail. Jackets. Jeans. A row of 'Hands Off' T-shirts. He's conscious of the Lyric white towel. His unpumped chest.

Paige Melder flashes him a smile. 'It's all been a bit rushed. Your manager squeezed me in because I've been following you for a while. I'm really grateful. I've been keeping genned up on you and I didn't think I'd be this lucky to actually get to talk to you. Not now it's going so well.' She keeps pouring out praise, drowning him in words.

'How come you've been following me?' he manages at last.

'I spent some time working on the local paper in Newton. I did a couple of articles when Kris Kowper did those original auditions there. I'm London-based now though. Here's my card—just so you know I'm genuine.'

Elliot glances at the card and tucks it behind the mirror, next to Anna's 'Good Luck' collage. She gave it to him last week, after he told her he'd got her and a mate on the guest list for tonight—it's a magical burst of stars cut out of green triangle sweet foils. He packed it before he left, alongside the spare frets and guitar strings. It felt special—a sort of talisman.

He turns back to Paige Melder.

She must be OK if she was in right at the beginning, but he still wishes Kris had let him know. He's on in two hours, and he wanted more time to run through the set. That face in the mirror looked calm enough on the outside, but inside he's racing adrenalin. He's starting with 'Trust Thing' but wonders now if it would be better to set the mood with 'Light A Candle'. And is 'Song for Insomniacs' right for the halfway break? Kris reckons it is and they've rehearsed it like that, but maybe . . .

Paige Melder pulls out a notebook from her jacket pocket.

'Sit down.' He nods towards the couch, which is the only place to sit. 'I can call for coffee.'

'Not for me.' She crosses her legs and clicks the end of her pen. 'I need to get through as quickly as I can.'

He goes to the shower room and pulls on the black HANDS OFF robe that he usually slobs about in before it's time to get changed. At least he's decent now. He walks back in and stands by the clothes rail.

Paige Melder watches him as he passes. 'Explain the HANDS OFF logo.'

Elliot hesitates. 'It's a kind of message. To show I'm focusing on my work.'

'Meaning?'

'Well—' he shrugs. He hasn't been asked stuff like this before. It's normally more to do with how he got started, and what his birth sign is. There have been a couple of interviews that have been more serious, but they've leant to the technical side. Musician material. This is something different. What would Kris want him to say? 'It flags up that I'm not available. To girls.'

Paige Melder's smile flashes again. '*Completely* unavailable?'

'Well . . .' He is thinking about Anna.

'Surely that's a struggle? A beautiful boy like you?'

He has to be careful here. Cautious. He picks at the sleeve of his robe, and then freezes. Dad does that when he's getting screwed up. No way is he going down that road. Dad is his warning light. Everything to avoid. 'It's the songs that matter. The music. I'm putting all of that first while I get started.'

Paige Melder scribbles this down. He can see her writing, black spiders on the page. 'So your energy goes into your creativity? All that frustration. It must make you very prolific.' That smile again.

'It's pretty tiring, being on tour.' He can feel his answers shrinking back from her, trying to lie low. He doesn't want this stuff in an article. It'll make coming clean to Anna even tougher. He should be telling *her* first. What if she sees it before he gets to her? He should've told her where to stand tonight, to make sure she gets the best view.

Paige Melder is watching him carefully. 'You must get lots of offers though?'

'It's all new for me. I'm just getting the hang of it.' He gets the feeling she's weaving webs. Why the hell did Kris book in an interview like this?

And then suddenly the door springs open and Kris is there. 'Everything OK?'

Elliot nods towards Paige Melder. 'An interview.' He takes the card out from behind the mirror, accidentally knocking Anna's star collage so that it slides down the back of the gilt frame.

Kris flicks a look at the card, then turns to the reporter. 'Who let you in?'

'Nobody stopped me.'

Elliot notices she's not smiling now.

Kris sighs. 'Security's obviously rubbish. I'll have to check that sort of detail myself in future.' Then, with a straight look at Paige Melder, 'The interview's over. You shouldn't even be here.' He taps the card. 'I could complain.'

'Only to me. I'm freelance.' She glances back at Elliot. 'I'll get you some other time, perhaps.' Then she leaves, her stiletto heels stabbing away down the corridor.

'She—she reckoned she had an interview booked. Said she knew you. From those first auditions.'

Kris squints at the card more closely. 'God knows. I've never met her. May have done a phone interview with her. It's hard to remember specific journalists—there've been so many. And I swear I didn't fix up an interview for this afternoon. She made *that* up, so maybe the rest was a story too.' He sighs again, shaking his head. 'I'm sorry. She should never have got to you. I need to look after you better.'

'Isn't she for real then? Some kind of fraud?'

'Oh, she's real, all right. But it's the sort of reality we want to stay away from. My guess is she's a tabloid journalist—and from the scummier end. Gets her stories through the back door—pretty well literally, in this case. And if she *is* the sort of reporter I think she is, if she gets even a sniff of a bit of dirt on you, there's a chance she'll be blowing her nose all over the front pages of whatever rag she can flog it to.'

'Nice.'

'No. Not nice.' Kris looks round the dressing room, as if he is checking for hidden bugs. 'Not nice at all.'

Elliot watches him for a moment, and then remembers Anna's collage. He goes across and picks it up, holding it at arm's length. It feels tainted somehow. Damaged, because of the back-door journalist.

'Who made you that?' Kris's eyes latch on to the picture, and he frowns.

'Just a mate.' Elliot tries to smooth down the corners that got crumpled as it slid. There's dust on it too, and a long grey cobweb caught against the foil.

Sweeping cobwebs
from his eyes
he saw her spidered scrawl
of crawling
lies.

Chapter Twenty-Six

Anna walks into the Lyric with Lucy, both of them trying to keep their faces still. Both of them trying to look older than they are.

Lucy nudges her. 'Shall we get a drink?'

Anna nods. 'Bacardi Breezer. Passion fruit.' She'd had the 'I'm trusting you so don't let me down' lecture from Mum, but one drink isn't going to hurt. And she needs it. She's probably more knotted up than Elliot is backstage. But at least she's here. She'd had to let Lucy in on the secret, but they've been best friends for ever, and she knows it won't go any further.

They stand together at the bar, Anna looking at the posters on the wall behind. They're mostly people she's never heard of, and that makes her feel even worse—as if she's lived her life in a shell. She wants to be here—she begged Mum to let her be here—but she feels wrong now, out of place in this noisy hall, more than half the audience female and fantastic looking.

It's not a huge crowd but Elliot said it probably wouldn't sell out. It's just a kind of a warm-up gig. Trying to get him some good reviews, and getting his name known.

'What would you like?' The girl who serves them is pretty—no, beautiful—with spiked razor hair and a china doll face.

Anna wonders if she knows Elliot. Do they all get together before a gig? After a gig? All the amazing people he must be starting to spend time with—he's not really going to stay interested in her for long. The thought of this is like a shadow. She made him a picture—a collage out of green foil sweet wrappers. It took her forever to get it right, but she feels stupid now. She's always making him pictures or paintings or candles and things, but she ought to stop. It's too young. Too girlie.

'There you go.' Lucy slides the drink over to her and touches her arm. 'Shall we go and stand near the front, before it gets too crowded?'

'God no!' Anna nearly spits out the Bacardi in her shock.

'Why not? He'll be able to see you then.'

'Exactly.' Anna takes a bigger slug of drink than she'd meant to. 'We'll—or at least I'll—look stupid. Like I'm really keen and pathetic. And I'll feel like a groupie.'

'OK.' Lucy's agreement is one of the things Anna loves about her best friend. She gives her loads of space. She's always there, but she never intrudes. And she's not a bit gossipy or bitchy like most girls at school.

They stand halfway back.

There's only a thin sprinkle of people between them and the stage, and she's watching a tall bloke checking the amps and the sound. All for Elliot. Elliot's world. And only a few months ago he was just someone singing in a car park.

She sips the Bacardi again, finishing it before she realizes how fast she's drinking. She'd better slow down. She's only ever really been drunk once before and she was sick all night and it was disgusting. No thanks. Never again.

Excitement bubbles through her suddenly, the shadow lifting. It's amazing all this really. Whatever happens with her and Elliot, she's at least here tonight, watching him right at the beginning.

And if he gets big—really really big—and leaves her behind, she'll just have to end up sitting in pubs getting hammered on passion fruit Bacardi Breezers and rattling on about 'how I used to know Elliot Heath. Honestly. Right at the beginning, before it all happened for him.'

'I'll get you another drink.' Lucy breaks into the fantasy. 'Same again?'

'Just one more, then I'll move on to water.'

'Me too.' Lucy edges her way back to the bar, and Anna stays standing on her own, trying to ignore a bald bloke—loads older than she is—who keeps winking at her. She notices that the straggle of people in front is moving nearer to the stage. It opens up a space around her but she can't bear to move forward. She still couldn't handle the idea of being close to where he is.

But the knots in her tummy are tightening and

twisting again. He's coming on. He's coming on.

And there he is—right there—standing in the centre of the stage. He looks out at the crowd, lifts his hand and nods in a sort of half greeting. She can't tell what he's thinking. What he's feeling. Hands off. Untouchable. She can see why it works. The crowd presses tighter. He is still just standing, looking. She thinks then that perhaps she *should* have gone closer. Perhaps he's looking for her. And the next minute he's hitting in with 'Trust Thing', which he wrote the day he bought her the green triangles and she suddenly doesn't feel so stupid about the collage any more. He told her the song was a present to her, and she said the picture was a present back. They give each other the best things they can. There's nothing pathetic about that.

'Oh my God!' Lucy is back by her shoulder, handing her the new Bacardi. 'Is that him? He's gorgeous! Are you really—'

'Ssssssh!' Anna feels her face burn.

'Sorry—I didn't mean—no one would guess from me blabbing that out, would they? Oh God, sorry.' Lucy squeezes Anna's shoulder. 'Sorry sorry sorry. Me and my big mouth.'

'It's OK.' Anna finds herself starting to giggle. She feels flushed and excited and suddenly proud, nudging closer to Lucy and whispering, 'But yes—I am *really*.'

Lucy nudges her back, giggling too. 'Then you're a lucky cow.'

Anna turns away, her eyes fixed on Elliot. She's

glad—relieved—that Lucy knows. Glad she can share some of it with her. Although she'll still have to be careful. She won't risk telling even Lucy anything really private.

But Lucy's right. He's gorgeous gorgeous gorgeous.

And when Lucy links her arm, and drags her to the edge of the stage, she goes.

WELCOME *to the website of*

Elliot

Touch the Untouchable

Elliot announces UK tour dates
view info >

Single 'Untouchable' out 18 April
view info >

Join the mailing list here
view info >

1st Album 'Trust Thing' out 21 April
view info >

Click here for video download!

what's new? | back stage | noticeboard | library | members | get stuff | tour info

MUSIC MAKER

Touch the Untouchable

ELLIOT – A Star Rising

Getting to know you . . . in which the up-and-coming voices of today talk to Susie Clarkeson and reveal their earliest influences.

There's something fiercely compelling about the newest heart-throb in pop. And it's not just the gritty, hauntingly raw voice. Take in the dark, unfathomable eyes. The ruggedly beautiful face. He handles complex mixes with maturity and sensitivity, and the songs throb with addictive riffs and a sweeping soundscape. Yet alongside this gift of sound, Elliot emanates a warmth and vulnerability that draws the crowd in. This is a combination that will stretch beyond the moment, and current music trends. This is a combination that will last.

We caught up with Elliot after a breathtaking performance at the Rose Bowl in Stoughton.

What's your all-time favourite album?

'Driving Seat' by Marc Wild. He's my hero. I guess you could say I cut my teeth on him—and on the title track off that album.

Which musician, other than yourself, have you ever wanted to be?

Do I need to answer that? Marc again, of course. Although I could chuck in a bit of Bobby Lewis and I love the voice of Hank Heeley from Skunk Fudge.

What, in terms of your music career, would you most like to happen next?

Phew. Don't know. I'm just trying to take things one step at a time. The single's doing well, and we've got the album release at the end of April so, to be honest, that's heady enough for me at the moment. I never even expected to get this far, and if it all blows away tomorrow, I guess it'll still have been worth it.

Not that we can see that happening! (Ed.)

Elliot's first single 'Untouchable' is out on the Obelisk label.

Next week's 'Getting to Know You' slot features Declan Barrett of Sabotage.

Chapter Twenty-Seven

'Listen to the birds. They're everywhere. Even this late in the afternoon.'

Elliot listens, and the air is full of singing.

Anna tugs at his hand, dragging him among the gravestones. An angel stares blankly down at him, a thin crack running the length of its marble face. He wishes Anna hadn't brought him here today.

Boris ambles up and cocks his leg against the carved swathes of white skirt. Or is it a gown, or a robe? Elliot isn't quite sure how to describe what angels wear. Maybe that's a song? Lyrics press in on him from everywhere. Some days, now, his head feels as if it will explode. All the ideas spilling out. Bits of words and tunes spinning up through the air. He's got to get that album together by the end of February.

He turns to Anna, who has her back to him and is tutting at Boris, clipping his lead back on. He's telling her today. He MUST tell her today. A mass of stuff has happened since the radio airplay. There were queues halfway down the street when he went to the HMV signing—and nearly a riot when they ran out of freebies. And on the back of that there've been letters and phone calls, and always a huddle of girls outside the house.

'I need to get you away.' Kris was insistent. 'Your single's out next week and things could go crazy then. I've got an apartment in London—I own a bit of property up there. One of my tenants is just about to move out—I can move you in within two weeks. We'll try and keep it private. And anyway, I need you closer. There's so much to do.'

'I'm not scared of the dead.' Anna squints up at the angel, yanking at Boris who is trying to wrap his lead round her legs. 'There's a girl at school who says she can see them. Ghosts, I mean. She says they are everywhere, all the time. She says when you talk about them, they draw closer. I wish I could see one.'

'I'd crap myself,' says Elliot. He looks at her, still looking up at the angel. She's got her hair up again and the lowering light of the sun touches the escaped strands, making a frizzed halo round her head.

'Come on.' Anna smiles, catching him looking at her. 'Let's walk.'

They leave the main path. A single brave daisy straggles up out of a mound of stones.

'Life,' says Anna. 'It's so wonderful. We mustn't pick it.'

Elliot watches her touch the petals and walk on. Soon, this evening, he is going to hurt her. He is going to pull off her petals one by one. He loves me. He loves me not. He loves me. He loves me not.

'Look at this headstone—it's beautifully carved. Two people buried here.' She leans across and clears the ivy from the inscription. 'Gilbert Price, Died in Action

June 1944. And Edith Price. Passed peacefully away December 2001. That's fifty-seven years apart. Do you think she still loved him all that time?'

Elliot shakes his head. It would be terrible if she did, and terrible if she didn't. 'Dunno.' He doesn't want to be thinking like this.

'Come on.' Anna sighs, reaching for his hand. 'I can see you're not into this. Let's go down the hill a bit. I used to play over there—that bit where they're building those houses. It was all woods and fields once.'

They skirt the iron fence that guards the dead, and slush down the muddying path and into the building site. She lets Boris off his lead again, and he scuds ahead, mud smattering up all round him.

The new houses are skeletal.

'Maybe there are ghosts from the future too.' Anna leans her head on Elliot's shoulder as they walk. 'Maybe they're watching us now. From the windows.'

Elliot moves away from her, bends to pick up the stick Boris drops on his trainer. As he throws it he glances sideways at the blank eyes of the houses. He pictures whole ghosted families drifting between the walls. There is someone cleaning in the kitchen. Someone singing in a front room. A hollow-eyed boy huddles in the garden, mashing out a tune on a toy guitar, while a blackbird sits on a branch above. There are shouts and something breaks in the kitchen. The singing stops. The hollow-eyed boy plays faster, his fingers blistering on the thin wire strings. He plucks out an eerie muddle of notes that mingle with the harsh warning cries of the bird.

Anna takes his arm again. 'Are you OK?'

'I need to tell you something,' he says.

'You've met someone else. Someone beautiful and talented and wonderful?'

He looks at her. What the hell is he throwing away? But it's not fair to lead her on. He loves me, he loves me not. He loves me, he loves me not.

The afternoon light is fading, and a creeping dark begins to fuzz the edges of the bushes and trees.

'I'm not supposed to have a girlfriend.' It sounds stupid when he says it. A hollow-eyed boy not being allowed to go out to play.

'What d'you mean?'

'Girlfriends. I've agreed not to have one. In that contract.'

Boris gallops back and drops another stick. Elliot picks it up. Throws it. He has mud on his hands.

'That contract was weeks ago. Since then we've got . . . closer.'

He closes his eyes. Shakes his head. 'That's the trouble. Too close. I can't risk it.'

She stops walking, her face cold marble. 'You've used me.'

'It wasn't like that.'

Boris bounces up with the stick again, but this time Elliot doesn't take it. A dove calls from over in the graveyard. 'Sorry,' he says.

'How long?' she says quietly.

'What d'you mean?'

'How long can't you have a girlfriend for?'

'Two years. While I'm getting started.'

She is staring at him, thoughts shifting like clouds across her eyes. 'So that's why I wasn't allowed to tell my friends about you.' It is a statement. Not a question.

'I . . .'

'And that's why I've never been to your house. You've only ever got me into one gig. And you never ask me to come with you to the studio.'

'I . . . we can still be mates. I want us to be mates.' He is clumsy. Pathetic. Weak as a daisy.

'Oh, great.' Her eyes suddenly clear. 'You mean when you've got some spare time, or you've had a bad gig, or you're just feeling low, you might text me. Or ring me. Spare me precious minutes of your superstar time.' Her face crumbles then, and she turns, running back along the lumpy road and up the hill into the graveyard.

Boris bounds after her, his tail waving wildly. He stops just once, turning back to look at Elliot with a puzzled gaze, then lollops on to catch her up.

In the fuzzed trees and bushes there are still birds singing. The graves on the hill are touched with gold.

Elliot stands statue still, a thin crack running the length of his heart.

Truth bleeds from stone.

Never felt so

alone.

WARWICK ARTS CENTRE

February 12TH

The Untouchable

Elliot

'There are very few singers today who have the depth and individual character within their voice that enables listeners to identify with the artist even if they've never heard the songs before. Newly discovered Elliot Heath is undoubtedly one of those singers.'
(MusicMaster review, Jon Audain, Jan 14)

TICKETS £10.00
(£17.50 on the night)

Doors open 7.30p.m.

Come and be touched . . .

Chapter Twenty-Eight

Elliot waits in Fat Tuesday's. A seat near the door.

A couple of girls have glanced at him, but he hasn't been recognized. Not yet. The jazz scratches at him. It's too loud and too fast. The table he's chosen is ringed with the remains of someone else's coffee. He knows he shouldn't have come, but he needed somewhere to pick up the taxi, and clawing in the back of his head is the wild idea that Anna might come looking for him. He's being stupid. A dog that won't leave the stick alone. And even if she came, nothing could change. They'd say the same words. Have the same fight. Again and again and again.

He sips at his coffee, then puts the cup down. It's too strong. Too bitter. He should take it back, but he can't be bothered. He wants to drop his head down onto his arms, squeeze his eyes and his ears shut, block out the glancing girls and that scratching buzz of jazz.

But he won't be able to block out Anna. Is she back at home, chucking candles in the bin? Burning all those sketches? How long will it take her to get someone new? On the table opposite there is a man and a little curly headed boy. The boy is giggling. Then he looks across, his eyes catching Elliot's. Whatever he sees there makes him stop laughing and bury his face in the folds of the man's sleeve. Elliot looks away, out through the window. His reflection stares back at him, merging with the people hurrying through the evening streets. Another ghost.

'Taxi? For Elliot Heath?' A bite of iced air gulps in through the café as the driver pushes his head round the door.

The glancing girls stare harder, the name sinking in. Their eyes boggle. They nudge each other. One of them stands up and starts to come over. Elliot leaves the too bitter coffee and follows the driver outside.

'Westhill Road?' The driver is watching Elliot in his rear-view mirror. He has to say it twice before Elliot answers because he has turned away, watching Fat Tuesday's until they round the corner and it is gone.

'Yeah. Number 33.' He thinks of Anna in the graveyard. And angels. Blinking the memory away, he stares out through the windscreen. Slow lines of brake lights burn red in front of them. He's got to look ahead. The music's got to come first. There are two gigs at the weekend. A radio interview. More store promotions. He won't have time to think. He won't have time to feel.

Except he's feeling now.

When his mobile bleeps it is like a song-burst. He

scrabbles in his pocket, sees the tiny envelope symbol on the screen. A text message. His hand shakes as he punches the button, reads what she's said.

'WHAT U DOING?'

'AM IN A TAXI.'

Seconds pass. Minutes. The traffic begins to clear and they are on the motorway, spinning down the fast lane. Weaving behind lorries. The taxi driver is an ex-Formula One driver. Or a nutter.

Elliot's mobile bleeps again. 'WHERE U GOING?'

'BACK 2 WESTHILL.'

'MEET ME.'

'OK.'

'WHERE?'

'WHITE HART. OGDEN STREET.'

There is a pause. He wonders if he should call her, but he's scared he'll mess it up and say the wrong thing. Does she know where Ogden Street is? He chose it because they're OK about him in there. It's a live music venue and no one hassles him. They're used to famous faces. But how will Anna get there? He thinks he could get the driver to turn round, come off at the next junction and go back to her place, but as he leans forward to ask, her answer flashes back, 'I'LL B THERE.xx'

Elliot is in love with the taxi driver now. His speed. His nerve. That's what you need in a driver. A bit of attitude. Someone who's going to get you there, come what may. He suddenly remembers the gravestone. Edith Price and whoever her husband was. Fifty-seven years. And suddenly two years doesn't seem so bad. Could he ask Anna for that?

He scrolls back to the last message. 'I'LL B THERE. xx'

He reads it again and again. Those two kisses. Whatever happens, it's going to be OK. And then he reads the number running along the top of the screen. The number the texts have been coming from. He sits, staring down at the message again. The words look different suddenly. Impostors. Invaders. He glances up as a lorry blasts its horn, its headlamps flashing fury. An insect hits the windscreen and the taxi driver washes it off, the wipers smearing the smudge of its exploded body across the glass.

Elliot's eyes drop back to his mobile again. The number is not Anna's. It's Amber's. All his senses slump and drain. He hasn't seen Amber for ages—not since she dropped out of college and became some sort of groupie for Sabotage—and based on all the gossip and rumour that's been flying round about her, he doesn't want to. But whatever he thinks of her, he can't leave her waiting at the White Hart.

He flicks on the 'reply' button, about to call her back and tell her he can't make it after all, when he gets a sudden picture of himself going home. He'll have to deal with Dad. Deal with sitting on his own up in his room. Deal with his mobile that isn't going to bleep. The White Hart is at least somewhere to kill the evening. It doesn't much matter who he sits through it with. Amber is as good—or as bad—as anyone.

Killing the night,
Just to feel all right.

Chapter Twenty-Nine

Amber can't decide whether to wait inside or outside the White Hart. In the end she chooses outside. If she goes in she'll have to order, and she wants Elliot to do that for her. And anyway, she's already had two vodkas, up the road at the Elm Tree. She needs to pace herself a bit.

She stands near the side of the door, underneath the streetlamp. The glow from the light will be spilling down on to her hair. Touching it flame gold. He always liked her hair.

The taxi slides up and she watches him lean forward to pay the driver. He looks different. But amazing. As he climbs from the car she steps forward and hugs him. Old friends. Old lovers. He needs to know that touching is OK.

'Hi.'

'Hi.'

He looks round nervously, as if he is scared of being caught out at something. Maybe he is. Scared of being spotted by his little girl fans. Scared of his photograph being snapped and appearing on a dubious front page. The idea excites her. Although it's dangerous. It was a dubious photograph that caused all the trouble with Declan—someone sent it to his wife.

She links her arm through his. 'Shall we go in? Have a drink?'

'Yeah. Sure.'

'I can't stay long.' He doesn't exactly look lit up about seeing her, and she decides she needs to cool off towards him a bit. To let him know this is a casual thing that's come up because she's just passing through. It isn't true, of course, but she isn't about to let him see that her plan is to spend the whole evening with him. Maybe the whole night. Mum's away again, and her sisters can get stuffed. They probably won't even come home anyway. But she's got to keep in mind another of her rules. Girls must never seem to make the first move.

They push open the door and go into the pub. It's too early for it to be throbbing—there's just the barman, and a couple of old blokes with newspapers. The barman gives the thumbs up to Elliot, but the old blokes don't even look up. Amber skims the headlines:

SEX SHAME OF SAUCY SOCCER STAR

PORNO PICS OF PALACE PARLOUR MAID

Dubious front pages.

Dubious old blokes.

It's a shame there are no girls in the bar. That used to be something else that excited her. Whenever she went somewhere with Elliot, girls would make cows' eyes at him and then slide their gaze over to her. She could see them trying to discover how she'd hooked a catch like that. It wasn't hard to work out, and they'd look away quickly. No competition.

She lights a cigarette, offers one to him.

'No thanks. It does my voice in.'

'Sorry, I forgot.' She thinks she ought to stub hers out, then decides it's best not to look as if she's trying too hard. And anyway, she needs this prop for now. She's more nervous than she thought she'd be. She draws on the cigarette slowly, her cheeks hollowing.

'What you drinking?'

'You need to ask?' She slides her smile at him, holding him with her eyes.

He turns to the barman. 'Vodka and ice. And a pint of lager, please.'

They take the drinks and sit at a table which is pock-marked with cigarette burns. The silence feels awkward. She needs to fill it. She has to remind him how well they get on, and how much they've got in common. 'I've been on the road. With Sabotage.'

'I know. I heard.'

The door opens and a couple come in. They are pressed against each other, all lovey and sloppy. She sees Elliot look round at them. Raw pain crossing his face. He used to watch her, his dark eyes following her everywhere—even when they were finished. Especially when they were finished. She'll have to go carefully and not push too fast. He won't want to risk her knocking him away again.

'So—aren't you going to ask me about it?'

'About what?'

She raises her eyebrows slightly. He's game playing,

but these are rules she understands. 'Sabotage. Being on the road.'

He seems to struggle to pull himself round to the question. Maybe he's battling with the idea of her being around a band like that. 'How was it?'

She curves her lips upwards, smiling into him again. She needs to keep the jealousy stabbing for a bit longer, but flatter him too. Give him some control. 'It's another world. Fantastic. You're so lucky to be getting into it.'

He has his arms on the table and she does the same. Not exactly a rule, but a useful tactic—mirroring people's actions is a way of making them think you've really tuned into them. 'One night—the band were doing a gig in Manchester—and Declan decided he wanted a curry after they'd come off stage. You met Declan, didn't you? That night at The Edge?'

'Yeah.' Elliot nods, then seems to force himself to add, 'He was good.'

She wants to laugh and add *very good*, but holds back from it. She needs Elliot to think he is the best person ever. The one and only.

'So anyway—the curry. He didn't want *any* curry. He wanted a curry from the Indian Garden—his favourite curry house in London.' She waits for the reaction. It doesn't come. She sips more vodka, feeling it burn through her. 'So guess what he did?'

'Sorry?' He has turned to watch the sloppy 'in-loves' again.

'Guess what Declan did. About the curry.'

'Oh—yeah. I dunno. Drove to London?'

'Nope. Better than that. He got Terry—that's their manager—to ring up and order it. It got couriered halfway across England. It took over four hours.' She has his attention now, although she can't read his expression. Hands off. Untouchable. She can see why everyone's going nuts about him.

'It must've been cold,' he says.

'Yeah, that's the real joke.' She drinks more vodka. Lights another cigarette. 'By the time the curry reached us we were all out of our heads and no one wanted it. We emptied it inside a hotel pillow, then Declan sneaked into Liam's room—he was off with some girl somewhere at the time—and emptied it on his bed.'

'You were doing drugs?'

She rolls her eyes, then giggles. 'We all did it. I can get you some if you want.' Lifting her hair slowly she lets it splay out through her fingers, tumbling down over her shoulders. She has to keep him noticing.

'I don't want. I don't do drugs. They screw you up—not just you but people round you.'

She stops the hair splaying quickly, and curls just one strand round her finger. A little bit nervous. A little bit insecure. 'No—you're right. I'm glad you're not into it. I only tried it a couple of times—just because it was there. Pathetic really. I was way out of my depth.'

The smoking was one thing, but she has to backtrack on this. She remembers now that he was always hung up about trying anything—said once he hated the thought of losing control like that. Still, it's a shame. Just a bit—even a taste—would loosen him up. She gets a mad idea that she could dust something into his lager when he's not looking. Just a sprinkle. She's got a capsule in her bag—it's neat powder so it wouldn't need much. Once he's seen how good it feels, she can come clean and maybe they can take it properly together. It will just be a laugh. No one will get hurt. And she won't be dragging him into a drug-fugged dangerous future.

She realizes he is still watching her, his face pale and strained. He's probably worrying about her. Wondering if she's really OK. She smiles—a proper smile, not planned. She's drawn him to her at last. She'd been beginning to think she had a job on her hands.

'So how come you're here?' he frowns. 'Sabotage are still touring, aren't they?'

She flips her mind through possibilities, wondering whether to go for the truth, and decides that she will. He's sensitive. She'll play for his sympathy.

'It all went wrong with me and Declan.'

'You started off with one of the roadies, didn't you?'

She's surprised he knows this. She had been, briefly, but Declan had come on to her, so obviously there was no competition. Not between a roadie and a lead singer. 'That was how I got to meet the band, but as soon as I saw Declan it was—well—it just felt right.

Have you ever sensed that with anyone?'

His jaw seems to tighten, and he shrugs. 'Maybe.'

She needs to be careful here. He's too proud to admit how he felt about her. How he still feels. But she has to plant the idea that she feels it too. She tilts her head slightly on one side. Another body language trick. The message is caring. Compliant. Available. 'Anyway, it was all wrong. With Declan.'

'Why?'

He's really listening now, but she's going to have to steer away from the full truth. She's not sure how he'd take the fact that after that anonymous photograph Declan's wife showed up and there was a scene and she was the one who lost out. She doesn't want to risk telling that one to Elliot, and she doesn't want to have to voice it herself. When she thinks about it, she still gets spiked with anger. Dick-head Declan. He didn't even stick up for her against the bitch. 'I realized there was someone else—someone I couldn't stop thinking about. I'd just been pretending with Declan.'

He gives her a slow look then, his words husked and sad. 'That must be tough.'

She tries to keep the edge of triumph out of her eyes. She knows he's saying he's been there himself. With her.

'So do you think . . .' She knocks back the vodka, then scrunches up the cigarette packet, squashing it down into the ashtray. It unfolds slowly. Like a beast that won't die. '. . . if something's really special but you mess it up, then you might get a second chance at it. A chance to put it right?'

He stares down at the unfolding beast in the ashtray, then looks up at her again. 'I hope so.' His voice is very soft. 'I hope so.'

Chapter Thirty

'Hi. Just checking in. Sorry I didn't call yesterday but it was so late by the time I got sorted. How you doing?'

There is a long pause and Elliot can hear the rasp of Dad's breath before he speaks. 'Yes. Thank you. Thank you very much.' Another pause.

'The apartment's not bad. Bigger than I'd expected.' Elliot doesn't want to sing and dance too much about the apartment to Dad. How can he tell him about the luxury cream carpet and leather chairs? The black laquered furniture? The shining white kitchen?

He was blown away when Kris brought him in yesterday, showed him round, explained about the heating and the video system and the intercom manned by security to make sure only the 'right' people get through. But now, picturing Dad picking at his sleeve in the dingy hall with the paint peeling off the wall and the tired frayed carpet, he feels himself slump.

He walks into the bedroom and sits cross-legged on the giant chrome bed. 'Dad . . . are you eating properly?'

'Yes, thank you. Thank you very much. Very much.'

'I stocked up the freezer for you. I told you that, didn't I? It's all stuff you like.'

'Thanks. Very much.'

Dad's voice sounds so distant. So frail. Elliot wonders if he's getting worse, or if just being away from him for these first two days has made him see Dad differently. He gets up again, paces the bedroom. Walks in, and then out, of the en-suite. 'I'm playing tonight so I haven't got too long to talk. Dad? You still there?' There is a long silence. Elliot feels his chest tighten with panic. 'Dad?'

'There's been a cat in the garden,' Dad says suddenly, his voice brightening. 'Big tabby. Keeps waiting by the door. Wailing.'

Elliot sits on the bed again and closes his eyes, wondering if he should leap in a taxi and go racing back home that second. They used to have a cat. A big tabby called Sheba. Dad put in a cat flap for her but she'd never use it. She'd just sit outside and wail. It was a family joke. One of the few. But that was years ago and Sheba had died of being old and they buried her down by the shed. Elliot made her a wooden cross out of lolly sticks and Mum laid flowers on the earth all round it. Was Dad hallucinating? He'd done that once before—not about cats, he kept seeing people then—but the doctor had changed his tablets and he'd been OK for ages now. But perhaps Elliot leaving had tipped him again.

'D'you think I should let it in? Feed it?'

Elliot rubs the back of his neck, then pushes his

hand through his hair. 'Sure. If you want to. I think you should worry more about feeding yourself though.'

Kris has organized for some woman called Beverly—a sort of home help—to go in once a day and check Dad out, and Elliot thinks he should ring her. Maybe she needs to go twice a day. He'll need to clear it with Kris, of course, but the extra expense would be worth it—for all of them.

He glances at the time on the digital radio. There's a car coming in half an hour and he's got stuff to sort out before tonight's gig. 'Look, Dad, I'm really sorry but I'm going to have to go. But don't worry about anything. We're looking after you—that lady I told you about will be in every day—and I'll be down before the end of the week. I promise.'

He'll have to clear that with Kris too. Kris wants him up here all the time. He's got a mass of things booked.

'I don't need anyone coming in. No ladies.'

Elliot thinks Dad is at least coherent on this subject. 'Just give it a try. It's only to help you out.'

'I don't need anyone coming in.'

Elliot can hear the shreds of panic in Dad's voice, razored by the thought that he might have to talk to someone he doesn't know. 'No. No. OK.' He keeps his own voice soothing. 'We'll go through it when I come down. And I'll ring you again tomorrow. I'll make sure it's about this time. So you know it's me.'

'So I know it's you.' The lost, losing-it Dad is back again.

'You take care now. Talk tomorrow.' The connection cuts dead. Elliot puts his mobile down next to the radio. He wonders if Dad is still standing there holding the reciever, or if he's already shuffling back into the front room to sit in the dark. Or maybe he's gone shambling round to the kitchen door to listen to the wailings of his imaginary cat.

Elliot gets up off the bed again, scanning the apartment, everything in it suddenly meaningless. He's lost Anna—it's been two weeks and he's held out against calling her, telling himself it's the right thing for both of them.

And Dad's losing himself.

The buzz of the intercom cracks across his thoughts. 'Hey there.' Kris's voice muffles through. 'You all ready? I've got a different car, because the girlies were starting to recognize the last one. But word's got out what time you're arriving at the gig, so I need to get you there early. Make sure they don't all leap on you.'

'Come up.' Elliot goes over and presses the switch that opens the door.

He stands by the window waiting for Kris to appear, looking down on a couple of business-suited blokes heading home in the late afternoon. A sleek young woman on the pavement opposite glances impatiently at her watch and clicks her fingers for a taxi. On Elliot's side of the road, a silver grey Daimler is parked by the 'permit holders only' sign, the chauffeur sitting patiently with the engine softly thrumming. Nobody even glances at it. Top of the range cars and chauffeurs are basic round here. He remembers a time of rattling buses.

Will he change? On the inside? Will this world of silver-grey Daimlers start to feel like his?

Dream your ghosts.
Scream silence down the phone.
Makes me think
I should be coming home.

WELCOME *to the website of*

Elliot

Touch the Untouchable

Return to home page

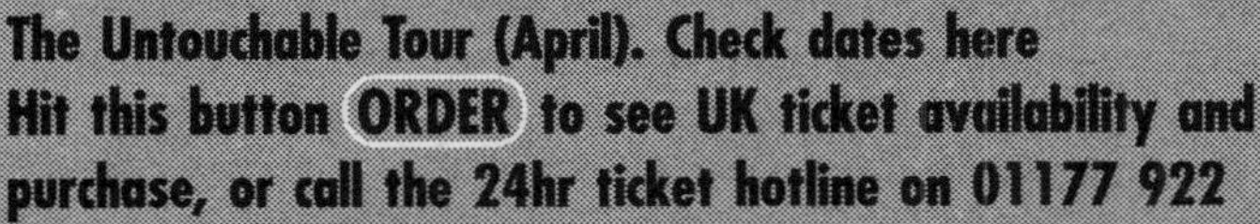

The Untouchable Tour (April). Check dates here
Hit this button ORDER to see UK ticket availability and purchase, or call the 24hr ticket hotline on 01177 922

21 April Exhibition Centre, Watchford
22 April Evening News Arena, Wigan
23 April Beaufort Theatre, Stockton-on-Trent
24 April Hallam Halls, Sheffield
26 April Bournemouth Bowl, Bournemouth
28 April Queen Elizabeth Hall, Guildford
29 April The Cave, London
30 April Palace Halls, Brighton

what's new? | back stage | noticeboard | library | members | get stuff | tour info

Chapter Thirty-One

The Rolls Royce nudges through the late-night streets, stopping and starting at traffic lights and people and once a small black cat that skimmed out in front of them.

'You don't see many cats in London.' The driver glances at Elliot in his rear-view mirror. Elliot hasn't had this driver before. Kris has organised a fleet of 'rollers' to ferry him about on this tour, and there's a different driver every night.

'No. I guess not.' Elliot watches the cat whisk away down a side road.

'Must mean good luck—though don't know if it's meant for you or me.' The driver laughs, the car purring as it pulls away from a crossing. 'Hope it's me—you seem to be lucky enough already.'

'Yeah. Must be meant for you.' Elliot tries to shake a short laugh back, but he always struggles with this 'journey home' banter. He can never bring himself down enough to focus. His head is always floating high, buzzing back over the gig. Wired on the memory.

But the driver is right about the luck thing.

This is what he's always wanted. Exactly where he wants to be. At the end of a gig he can block out most of the down-side which hooks him back to Mum and Dad and Anna. Especially Anna.

He puts his hand on the guitar, which is on the seat next to him, as if touching it will keep the luck flowing through him. The skin on his finger tips is blistering again. It was screaming sore as he played, but he had to keep going. Screaming sore fingertips are part of the package. Kris reakons they'll harden up soon. Toughen up. Roughen up. Like the rest of him. But, still, he needs to whack some cream on for now, for when he gets on stage tomorrow.

It was packed out again tonight. It's always packed out. He closes his eyes and can still see the blurred faces of the crowd. Hear his own voice in his head. The amp was a bit off, and Kris had a go at the sound guy, but mainly they rolled through it. By the second half, The Cave rocked. It was a good venue. Loads of atmosphere.

As he runs it through again and again, Elliot thinks that every gig ends before he's ready. Kris is hot on him keeping to the set list and sticking to two encores—maximum—but left to himself, Elliot sometimes thinks he could go on all night. He could outstay the audience and still be singing at sunrise, even if he was in there on his own.

The Rolls Royce stops. 'OK—you're home.'

Elliot's eyes jerk open. 'Thanks, mate.'

'No problem. You're in Brighton next, aren't you? Palace Halls? You're booked with us, though it'll be a different driver for that one.'

'OK.' Elliot nods, thinking he hasn't got a clue where they are next. Kris handles all that.

'All you have to do is write, sing, and play,' he'd said. 'I'll do everything else.'

Elliot opens the door and the driver comes round to help lift the guitar. 'Don't want to risk knocking this about,' he says.

'No. Thanks.' Elliot straightens up, then takes it back from him. It's a Vintage Martin—part of a promotional thing that Kris has set up. He's getting paid to play it. He wonders if the car firm has been warned how valuable it is.

'Goodnight.' The driver stands and watches Elliot walk to the apartments. It isn't until he's keyed in his code and the door has opened that Elliot hears him get back in the roller and drive away. He thinks that Kris will have told the driver to do this too. Told him to check that he gets in OK. It's a safe street, but Kris isn't going to risk getting him knocked about either.

He goes up the stairs. Inside the cream and leather of his rooms, he switches on the dimmer lights and opens the window. There is a gentle thrum of traffic passing. Occasional voices. The lights of planes are like touches of magic in the sky. Elliot wants the outside world in with him. He's still too wired to sleep.

He pulls a chair over to the window, drops his key-card and mobile on the table beside him, and sits down with the Martin. Closing his eyes, he feels his way across the strings, running through some new sounds. He likes messing with the structure too—what happens when you put the chorus first? What happens when you run the chorus underneath the verse, going for a more textured layering of lyrics? What about a change of style—a rap in the middle? It's pretty raw, the stuff that comes out of him this end of the night, and Kris never likes it when he tries it out in rehearsals—says it's too difficult for the fans—but he needs to do it. Needs to keep pushing at the edges of his own ideas.

Tonight he's going for something fragile. A thin sound that probably wouldn't stand up live. But maybe if they got a keyboard behind it, it would get a bit more depth. He might suggest it to Kris tomorrow at rehearsal . . .

His mobile bleeps.

Elliot lays the Martin down carefully, but his heart isn't careful. It's suddenly jolted because he's thinking—the way he's always somehow thinking—that this time it might be Anna. She might have decided just to get in touch. She might have decided just to say 'hi'.

He reaches for it and checks the caller. It's not Anna—but at least it's not Amber. Amber's rung a few times, but he never knows what to say. The third time she called he switched the tone off in mid-ring. It was a crap thing to do, but he just feels awkward with her. Uneasy. But tonight, the name on the screen is Mum. 'Hi.'

'Hello? Elliot?' She sounds nervous, as if she thinks

it might not really be him. Maybe she thinks someone's nicked his mobile. Or his voice.

'That's me.' He wonders suddenly if something's happened to Dad. 'Everything OK?'

'Yes. Fine. I know it's late, but I thought you'd still be up. Did the show go well?'

The Show. Elliot thinks Mum makes it sound like a musical. 'Yeah. Great.'

'Where did you play?'

'Place called The Cave. It's just the other side of town. Not too far.' The driving distances hadn't been too bad for the last few gigs, but earlier this week they were right up in Sheffield. They'd driven all night to get back from that one—they had to head straight to Bournemouth because of a radio interview there the next morning.

'Did you have a good audience?'

Elliot gets a picture of Mum's idea of a 'good' audience, everyone sitting in plush velvet seats clapping politely at the end of each number. But at least she's trying. She went crazy when he first left college—he didn't tell her, he just did it. But Kris went round and talked her through everything and somehow he came out alive. In fact, more than alive—she came up to London to see where he was living and almost seemed pleased when she saw the apartment. Or at least, relieved. 'Yeah. It was a good audience.'

'That's good.'

'Come and watch. We'll put you on the guest list.

You and Sheldon.' Six months ago, Elliot could never have let himself invite Sheldon along to anything, but it'll be OK. As long as Dad doesn't find out. And Mum can hardly come on her own.

'We'll do that. Are you playing in London again soon?'

'I'll get Kris to have a look.'

'Thanks.'

There is a long silence. Elliot thinks suddenly that this is a fragile moment. Mum agreeing to watch him do something she's fought against. Something that scares her. The idea of him ending up like Dad. His mind runs backwards. A memory he doesn't want. She was waiting for him when he got in from school, and there was a suitcase by the front door. 'Are we going on holiday?' he said.

'I'm going away.' She was looking at him and her eyes seemed to be begging him for something but he didn't know what. He looked away, down at his black polished school shoes.

'When are you coming back?' He remembers his voice seemed small and thin.

There was a silence. A gap.

'She's not.' Dad's voice was as small and thin as Elliot's.

Elliot hadn't realized Dad was there, leaning against the frame of the kitchen door. Or maybe using it to stop himself crumpling.

More silence.

'Go on, tell him.'

'Elliot—you must know—must have guessed,' Mum said softly.

He made himself look at her then. This wasn't real. They were playing a game or acting a play and they wanted him to remember his lines. 'Don't,' he said. 'Don't go. Please.'

Please. Please.

Mum looked round at Dad as if she was wavering, 'Maybe I . . .'

'No.' There was a new, angry edge to Dad's voice. 'Don't back out of it now. You'll only start it all up again tomorrow. Or next week. Don't put me through it again.'

Another gap. The house so still, as if it didn't dare breathe.

'All right.' Her voice, at the end, was a whisper. 'But I'll come back for you, Elliot. Once I'm sorted out.'

Dad turned. Walked away into the kitchen. Elliot pictured him standing there, staring out into the garden.

And this time it was Elliot who had an angry edge to his voice. 'No. I won't go away from Dad.'

And he never had. Not until now.

'Elliot? Are you still there?'

'Yeah. Sorry. I'm just knackered.'

'I'm not surprised. I—I'll let you go. I'm sure you've got another hard day tomorrow. I'll call you again in the week.'

'Yeah. OK. Night.'

He drops the mobile on to the carpet and picks up

the Martin. He is trying for the fragile sound again, but the mood has moved. A bike roars past in the safe street outside. Maybe a piano would work better than a keyboard? Though keyboards are better for touring. And he could bring in a cello for those really dark sound moments. But the whole thing is too weak. He needs to toughen it up. Roughen it up. Layer it through with sounds that bleed. He sits, the riff growing faster and fiercer, as the sunrise washes a sleepy yellow across the night.

Tomorrow in your suitcase.
Still couldn't quite believe
you'd really leave.

ITEM TITLE	PRICE	BIDS	PAYPAL	TIME LEFT
<u>Elliot sold out</u> 2 X ELLIOT TICKETS Palace Halls, Brighton **100%** feedback received	**£72**	**24**	P	**15 m**
<u>HANDS OFF</u> **<u>Elliot Heath 'Untouchable' Tour</u>** 2 X ELLIOT TICKETS Brighton (venue sold out) ***100% NO RESERVE AUCTION***	**£60**	**31**	P	**21 m**
<u>HANDS OFF UNTOUCHABLE Tickets (sold out)</u> 2 X ELLIOT at Brighton, Palace Halls. Standing tickets. Last chance to see phenomenal new artist on current tour	**£55**	**17**	P	**54 m**

Chapter Thirty-Two

'And now let's hear it for that fast-rising star—ELLIOT!' The presenter steps backwards on the stage and Elliot runs forward.

The sight of him catches in Anna's throat.

The roar of the crowd is electric. She wonders if every audience screams at him like this. Buzzed up and loved up and all on his side.

She hadn't wanted to come.

Lucy was apologetic. 'I feel like I have to go—it's not every day my sister hands out Easter presents like this. She's coming too, but she doesn't know about you and him. I haven't told *anyone* about it—I won't break that promise.'

'Thanks. Although I s'pose it doesn't matter now.'

Lucy carried on, 'And Jen thought she was giving me the best pressie ever, with these Palace Hall tickets. They're gold dust. I didn't dare turn them down, but I wanted to give you first choice. I can take someone else if you want.'

Anna thought about the someone else that Lucy might take. She pictured them both, being there in the audience in Brighton. Her sitting at home, drawing Boris in her bedroom.

'It's OK,' she'd said. 'I'll come. I'm over him anyway.'

Except she isn't.

As he breaks the first chord the whole hall heaves, everyone waving and whooping and dancing as if the world is going to end tomorrow and this is the last gig they'll go to ever. She is trying not to cry.

There is a line of fans pressed up along the front of the stage. Elliot told her once that sometimes the girls at the front chuck their knickers at him.

'That's sick,' she'd said.

'Kris reckons it's a compliment.'

As she watches him move into 'Trust Thing', she wonders if the girls bring the knickers specially. Do they pack them in their bags along with lipstick and a hairbrush? Are they their best knickers, or the big Auntie Doris Christmas ones that they're never going to wear anyway?

Why does he have to be so beautiful?

The whole song is like soft silk. He closes his eyes and the knicker throwers stretch their arms out towards him and sway.

'Come nearer. Up to the front.' Lucy's eyes are shining, nudging her from behind.

Anna edges forward slightly. Those hands stroking that guitar once stroked her hair. She will slip back in a minute. She'll hide in the loo or wait outside. She won't put herself through this very much longer. But the damage has already twined itself into her. She's done it to herself. A form of torture. Why why why did she think this was an OK thing to do?

A pair of Auntie Doris Christmas knickers spin

towards him, flopping down almost unnoticed on to the stage. And then he opens his eyes.

Anna knows he has seen her, and she knows then that she has been waiting for him to. And wanting it. The playing doesn't change. Nor his voice. Or his expression. But he sings straight to her, every word winding strings around her heart.

Chapter Thirty-Three

'Drive round again.'

The driver does a U-turn and edges slowly back along the road; Elliot, in a roadie's hooded jacket, scanning the faces of the fans.

'We shouldn't be out here. I reckon things could get sticky if they recognize you.'

Elliot pulls the hood up further over his face. 'Just a couple more minutes.' He doesn't really know what he's doing. Or what he's hoping for. Tonight, seeing her so close, was like a punch in the gut. And when he came off after the encore, he slipped away when Kris was busy with the equipment, getting the driver to crawl along the thronged streets.

They pass the main exit to the Palace once more. There's still a mass of people coming out. It's impossible. He's going bonkers. There's no way he'll find her here, and even if he does he won't be able to get to her. He'll have to ring her at home or go and camp on her doorstep. Why did she come? Why did she have to be standing there like that?

They stop as three boys step out into the road in front of them. The driver swears softly. Hoots his horn. Someone bashes the bonnet and a huddle of faces peer in through the window. Elliot hunches his shoulders and looks down quickly, pulling the hood forward as much as he can.

'I reckon that's it for me,' says the driver, pulling away again. 'It's not safe. This car sticks out like a sore thumb round here. I don't want one of these kids falling under the wheels. And, besides that, your boss would have me hung if he knew what I was doing with you.'

Elliot leans back, the soft leather of the rear seat creaking slightly. Maybe she wasn't even there. Just a ghost. The way she sometimes comes to him in his sleep at night. Or early in the morning, the feeling that she's in the room with him just in the moment before he wakes up. The dead ache always grips him, the sense of having lost something, before the real day floods in and he lets himself push her to the dark at the back of his mind again.

'Gig went well tonight?'

Elliot realizes the driver is making conversation. The least he can do is answer. The bloke's put himself out—and at risk—for him. 'Yeah. A good crowd. The amps howled a bit though. We had quite a bit of trouble with those.'

'Don't suppose anyone noticed. Too busy howling themselves—'

The driver is cut short by Elliot's explosive shout. 'Hey—there. On the left. Pull over can you!'

The adrenalin pumps through him when he's on stage, but he didn't ever know his heart could drum this fast. 'Can you reverse up a bit? To the bus stop. Those two girls.'

As they draw level he presses a button on the side of the door. The window slides down with a small soft whirr. What if she tells him to get stuffed? What is he going to say? 'Anna . . .'

She turns. 'Elliot.'

'Will you get in? Go somewhere we can talk?'

Anna glances at the two girls beside her. The younger one, freckle-faced and about Anna's age, is boggling at Elliot. 'You go,' she manages to splutter. 'Me and Jen will be fine. Won't we?'

The other girl—an older version of the first one—is opening and shutting her mouth like a fish. Anna panics a look at them both. 'I can't just . . .'

The younger one gives her a small push. 'Don't be wet, Anna. *Go*.'

Elliot opens the door, slides along the seat to make room. 'Thanks, mate.' His eyes meet the driver's in the rear-view mirror. 'I owe you.'

'Forget it—sometimes you've got to take a chance.' The driver noses the car into the flow of traffic. 'Been there myself. My wife took a bit of chasing. Before we got married, I mean. But we'd better get away from this lot. Where'd you wanna go?'

Elliot glances at Anna, who is stiff and pale-faced beside him, her hands clenched together in her lap. 'Anywhere. Just keep driving.'

What the hell is he going to say?

'Hi.' She says it first, smiling shyly, and shrugging, as if it's suddenly all too mad to be believed.

'Hi.'

'It's good to see you.'

'You too.'

The driver turns on the radio. Country and western. Someone's baby has left them in the cold.

'You all right?' Elliot's voice is husked from the gig. He probably stinks.

'Sort of. You?'

'Yeah. Sort of.'

'Your single. It's doing brilliantly.'

'Thanks.'

'You're on *Top of the Pops* next week, aren't you?'

'Yeah.'

They're so polite. Almost strangers. 'Who were those girls?'

'My best friend Lucy. And her sister. Her sister was the one who got us tickets.'

He looks back out of the window, the Palace disappearing behind a block of drab, weary-looking flats. They pass a scuffle outside a kebab house. In the stretch of shop doorways there are huddled blankets with people underneath. A stray dog, skewer thin, slinks down the pavement, then skitters away behind an overfilled skip.

'How's Boris?' Elliot says.

'Bonkers. As ever.'

The driver turns the radio louder. Sings along. His voice is flat, but somehow honest and soothing. No one is as pretty as the l'il girl back home.

'I've missed you.' Elliot hadn't known he was going to say this, but once it is said, he isn't sorry.

'I've missed you too.' She reaches through the space between them, touches his face. The air shrinks. He can hardly breathe. Why is he letting this happen? They'll just be back at the beginning again.

'Can we meet? I know it can't be like before. I understand all of it.' She is talking fast and low. Someone who can hear the drip drip drip of time. The driver's love waits for ever beneath that old gold moon. They slow down for traffic lights. Cruise down narrow, sleeping side streets where all the lights are off, and the dark hulks of wheelie bins guard the front doors like soldiers on duty. 'But—just—it's been so hard . . .'

He takes her hand, pressing her fingers. 'Yeah,' he says. 'We'll meet. But it's a battle getting back home these days. Can you come up to London?'

She squeezes him back. 'Just tell me when.'

'I'll text you. Next week. I'm not gigging then.'

'OK.'

The road opens out again. Gets busier. A coach overtakes them. Faces press against the back window, staring out. Young people. Elliot can see that some of them are wearing 'Hands Off' caps.

'I'll need to get back now. Kris will hang me up by one of my guitar strings if he finds out what I've done. And I'm supposed to be at an interview in the dressing room.'

'Sorry.'

'Don't be. The driver will sort you out once he's dropped me. Get you into a taxi. It'll all be paid for. OK?'

'OK.'

They don't speak again, but she leans her head on his shoulder and he slips his arm round her, pulling her close.

The car circles a roundabout, heading back the other way. The driver drums a beat on the steering wheel, singing about being lonesome. The moon that hangs over the city is unnaturally gold.

Shine on through the crazy night.
This lunacy
that blinds us with its light.

Dear Elliot,

I saw you at Bournemouth and you are funky fantastic fabulous and fit. All my friends fancy you, but none of them are as nuts about you as I am. Please write and send me a photo. Then I can gaze at it before I go to sleep at nite. Love you lots.

Hayley Kissinger

Chapter Thirty-Four

Elliot stands on the stage as cameras swing round him. Sophie fusses with his make-up while he watches his dancers run silently through the sequence, their lips mouthing the moves.

His dancers. *His* dancers. He can't believe they're here to back him up. In fact, there's a stack of people that Kris has signed up to work with them for this show. Someone separate for his hair. Someone to help with his clothes. A couple of guys to give extra support for the lights and stuff. Elliot hasn't had time to get his head round learning their names, but it's like a real entourage. *His* entourage. And Kris reckons they're going to start needing this level of back-up for other gigs too.

'Over to the left a bit,' somebody calls. The lights change. Purples and reds flood over him.

Sophie narrows her eyes. 'I'll just touch a bit more on the cheeks,' she murmurs.

'One two, one two.' A bearded sound engineer flicks him a grin. The lights dazzle yellows and greens.

A girl band—Heaven Scent—are just finishing on the stage opposite.

Elliot would like to meet them, although he hasn't a clue what he'd say. And anyway, they've been caught up with their own rehearsal since he got here. Maybe later. There must be a chance to catch up with the other performers later.

'Hi—I'm the presenter. Great to have you here.' Craig Harris comes over to shake his hand, blocking Elliot's view of the girls. He's smaller in real life. Everyone's always smaller in real life. 'Your single's fantastic. It's going great.'

'Cheers.' Elliot thinks he should probably say something more exciting and dynamic to a *Top of the Pops* presenter, but he can't think what.

'Just step three paces to the right.' A skinny bloke with glasses focuses with a hand-held camera. 'We're going to pan out on the count of five.'

Elliot has already run through 'Untouchable' three times, but there's so much to take in. His head feels full of flashing lights.

'Just take it easy.' Kris comes over, checking his watch. Nodding at nothing. 'Conserve yourself. We've got two interviews before you go on tonight. Big ones.'

Elliot thinks about big interviews. Big rooms. Big questions. Will he seem small to the interviewers?

A giant camera lowers its long neck, its square eye staring blankly. A modern dinosaur. People of the future will dig up its rusted steel bones.

'The other two performers are Bobby Lewis and Heaven Scent.' Craig Harris gives a thumbs up as one of the Heaven Scent girls edges past. He turns back to Elliot. 'Bobby's flown in from New York. He dropped everything once he was Number One. We're expecting him any minute.'

Beside him, Kris shifts and coughs. Suddenly restless. Elliot knows what he's feeling, and he's feeling it too. They are both picking the flesh off those two words. Number One. 'Untouchable' has stormed in. Blizzarded and tornadoed. It's blasted from nowhere up to number seven. But it's not enough. Kris says they need to hit first time. The square eye dinosaur raises its head and glides away.

'We've got The Sessions pre-recorded, and a Traci Maran video.' Craig Harris has a flashbulb bright smile. 'If you've got any problems . . .' He touches Elliot's shoulder, but a string-thin woman with a clipboard interrupts him.

'I need to check out the final line up.' Her voice is breathless.

'Sure. Sure.' Craig Harris shakes Elliot's hand again. 'There's a whole crew here to look after you. Just shout if you need anything.'

He nods at Kris, and is gone.

Elliot can't take in that tonight is actually going to happen. He isn't really going to be up on Stage Two while his image beams into thousands and thousands and thousands of homes all over the world.

'Hey.' A muscle-thick bloke lazes over, hand stretched out, smiling. He's in baggy jeans. A loose grey vest. Strange green eyes in a burnt brown face. It's the eyes that knock Elliot away. From the back he might be a builder. A technician. From the front he's a kind of God. 'I'm Bobby Lewis. Heard your single in the car coming across from the airport. Wow. And your voice. Fantastic range. I'd struggle with some of those notes.'

'Thanks.'

Bobby Lewis's own voice is deep toned, like an oboe. And as Elliot stands, awkward and uncertain what to say next, he gets a rush of warmth for Bobby Lewis. He's just flown in from America. Everyone must be wanting to grab a bit of him. But he's found the time to saunter across and say something good about 'Untouchable'.

Swept up by this, Elliot adds, 'Well done. For Number One,' and as he says it, he realizes he means it too. He doesn't want all this sizing up other musicians. Is that what it's really about? He gets a view of himself suddenly, hissing, Gollum-like, from behind a set of amps. And it doesn't feel good.

'We're having a bit of a party later. We've rounded up some of the crew, and Heaven Scent have signed up to it,' Bobby Lewis is saying. 'Just thought we'd need a bit of a blow out to celebrate. Could you make it? It'll probably run all night.'

Elliot wants to go. To touch that glitzed bright world that he's standing on the edge of.

'Sorry, no parties.' Kris's smile is knife sharp as he cuts in shaking Bobby Lewis's hand.

'I thought . . .'

Kris doesn't even glance at Elliot. 'We're on a

pretty tight schedule, and this kid needs to sleep sometime.' He does glance at Elliot now, and his voice softens. 'You're being interviewed here straight after you've done your bit on stage. I've got you booked in for a Swedish TV one running on from that, and then you're on a late night chat show. I reckon that'll be more than enough. We've got a live gig tomorrow, remember.'

'No worries. Some other time.' Bobby Lewis shrugs. 'Anyway—I'd better go and get sorted.'

And then he is gone. Elliot notices the tangle of wires that run from all the cameras and lights. The crew look stretched. Hollow eyed. A lot of them were here half of last night too, getting the studio straight for the show.

'You look gorgeous.' Sophie appears at his side, checking his hair, waving a stick of eyeliner. 'We just need to add some definition. Now don't move, or the pencil will poke your eye out.'

The glitzed bright world slips away.

Elliot wonders if it was ever really there in the first place.

I've got the moon,
just swapped it for my name.
The dealer said
it's just
the price of fame.

We chatted with Elliot Heath on 6 May

The enigmatic Elliot got us just wanting more when we caught up with him backstage at the *Top of The Pops* Studio

Below are just some of the highlights.
To **watch** the **full chat video:** **Go here** 

TOTP: You're being plugged as the next Marc Wild. How good does that feel?
Elliot: Marc's my hero so yes, of course it's a massive compliment. I'm trying lots of sounds out at the moment though, so hopefully I'm not going to get too pigeonholed yet.

TOTP: We want to know something about your 'Untouchable' video. We're told it's very unusual. Surreal. Who came up with the idea for that?
Elliot: The film people. I'd like to say I was involved with the whole process, but it's early days for me yet. I guess I've just got to trust the experts. I'm still finding my way through the whole business.

TOTP: Is it right that you're filmed inside a glass pyramid?
Elliot: Yeah—I was supposed to be like a work of art. You know—with security round it and everything. It's all shot inside a gallery, and there's weird paintings and statues and stuff like that everywhere.

TOTP: And the dancers? How do they fit in?

Elliot: They're done up to look like visitors to the gallery. There's hundreds of them. It got a bit scary at one point, because they all have to dance right up to the prism to try and find a way in. It started to wobble a bit.

TOTP: So—let's talk a bit about that 'Untouchable' image. Surely there's some secret girlfriend stashed away somewhere?

Elliot: No.

TOTP: Well, with the impact you're making, that won't last for long. Some girl's bound to smash through that glass, so to speak.

Elliot: I hope not. Broken glass isn't good. Someone might get hurt.

TOTP: Well—we wouldn't want that happening either, Elliot. So—thanks for your time. And remember—any single girls out there—he's still available . . . you've just got to find the way to get through that glass.

NEXT ⏩

Chapter Thirty-Five

'Hi, Anna. I wasn't sure if you'd be out of school yet, but I needed to ring you and . . .' Elliot sits dripping at the pool side. He wants the air to dry him off. The rehearsal studio got so sticky hot—at one point he thought he was going pass out—but the swim has cooled him down again.

'Elliot—oh, brilliant—hi.'

She sounds buzzed up to hear from him, as if he's the one person she's been waiting for. He has to get the bad bit over with straight away. 'I can't do next week. Kris has booked stuff up.'

'Again?'

'It's gone a bit hectic since *Top of the Pops.*' It feels more than hectic. Some days he feels as if he's spinning off the end of the world.

'That's good. For you.'

Elliot hears the flattening of Anna's voice over the mobile. He wants to tell her that he's desperate for them to meet up, but he knows he'll make a mess of it and his words will just sound lumped up and clumsy. *Sorry sorry sorry. Understand me. Everyone's clawing for pictures and interviews and bits of my hair. The album's racing up the chart. I need to pull off another two singles. I'm knackered. But I never stop thinking about you.* 'Maybe we could do the following Friday?'

'Maybe.'

There is a long silence.

Two girls saunter by, shimmering in sequinned bikinis. They're waiting for Ryan and Jack, but the Skunk Fudge guitarists are still rehearsing in the studio next to Elliot's. Waiting for Ryan and Jack doesn't stop the girls flashing sideways glances at him. It scares him. They scare him. He's not even sure why. Except that, with girls like that you wouldn't know—couldn't ever be sure—that they were with you because it was *you* they liked, and not the Fame bit. That's not how it is with Anna. She's real. She's been there from the beginning. She's on his side.

But they've still only hooked up a couple of times since that night after he saw her at the gig. A snatched afternoon in a West End café, him in dark glasses and another hooded top. She'd laughed at him then and made him take the hood down because she said she didn't want to go out with a monk. But he kept the glasses on, even though she said she hated not seeing his eyes.

And he's made it back to Newton once, squeezed her in with a visit to Dad so that Kris wouldn't suspect anything. He has to try harder. Really make it happen this time. 'I mean it. I'll sort something out. Something definite.'

She is quiet again. He fills the space with things

she might be about to say: *This isn't working. I've met someone else. Get lost.*

The shimmery bikini girls go over to the pool-side bar, flicking giggles at him as they order cocktails. When he glances back at them they don't look away.

'The following Friday—that's June the third,' Anna says.

'OK. I'll write it down. I'll tell Kris I've got to go to a wedding or something.' Although even as he says it, Elliot knows he won't get away with that. Kris has peered into every corner of his life.

'You know what day that is? The thirty-third?'

'Sorry?' Tiredness washes through him in waves.

Anna sighs. 'The third of June. Do you know what day that is?'

'Um . . . not sure.'

Silence again: *You're wasting my time. I've realized you're a geek anyway. I hate you.*

'My birthday.'

'When?'

'The third. Of June.'

'Oh God. Yeah. I knew. I'm sorry.' That wakes him up. Kris can peer and poke and prod and push, and it won't do any good. He'll be taking Anna somewhere amazing that night.

'Do you really mean it? That we'll go out then?'

'Yeah—I really mean it.'

'I'll tell my mum then. Only she normally arranges a family thing. I'll make sure she doesn't.'

'Yeah—that'll be good.'

The shimmering bikini girls are giggling harder now. They flick their hair a lot. Talk with their hands. Their eyes keep Elliot in view.

He'll book a table somewhere special—get a cab to bring Anna up to London and meet her at the restaurant. Or maybe even a hotel. As long as it's discreet. The apartment isn't private enough. Kris knows the codes and he springs up every hour of the day and night. 'Just checking you're OK,' he says. But Elliot knows that's not it. He's checking he's there. Behaving.

'Hey—Elliot . . .' Elliot looks round. Kris is standing watching him, leaning against the tinted glass door of the shower room. 'You need to get organized. Remember we've got a press conference this afternoon.'

'OK.' Elliot realizes he is jumping to Kris's command, guilty as a schoolboy, and something in him pulls against it. 'I won't be long.'

He waits for Kris to walk away, but he doesn't. He stays watching. Elliot gets the sudden urge to chuck the mobile at him. He lowers his voice to Anna. 'I need to go. I'll book something. I promise.'

'Really definitely cross your heart promise?' The sweetness he loves her for is back in her voice.

He shoots a look at Kris, who has his head slightly cocked and his eyes narrowed, as if he is listening for cosmic vibrations. Except, of course, he isn't. He's trying to catch snatches of Elliot's conversation. 'Yeah. Thanks then. Text you later. Bye.' He follows

Kris into the shower room. 'I'll just have a rinse down.'

'Sure.' Kris is checking his own mobile for messages. 'I'll wait here for you.'

Elliot lets the iced spray sluice down over him, goose pimpling his skin. They've got everything here, at Obelisk studio. It blew him away the first time he came to record. The pool. The bar. A squash court and gym. And fantastic studios. Gold microphones. Almost.

'What's after the press conference?' Elliot wraps his towel back round him and steps out of the shower, trying not to sound rattled.

'We've got a night off tonight, so I've booked a restaurant. You, me, and a bloke who's flown over from Ireland specially to meet you.'

Elliot thinks that a bloke flying over from Ireland doesn't exactly sound like a night off. 'Who is it?'

'He's in television advertising. A friend of mine.'

'Advertising? Like TV commercials?'

'Yep.'

Elliott takes some cream from his wash bag, rubbing it into his blistered fingers. 'That'll cost us, won't it? A telly ad?'

'It's not you we're selling. Or at least, not directly. It's a Mercedes car campaign. They want to use "Untouchable" in the background.'

Elliot hesitates, screwing the lid back on the cream. 'Is that a good thing?'

'It's an excellent thing. But it's not all.'

As Elliot zips his jeans he realizes Kris's face has that wired-up look it gets when it's been a good gig, or a good interview. 'What else?'

'They want you in it. Driving the car.'

'What?' He stops, his fly only half up, then shakes his head. 'That's not me. I'm not an actor. And I don't drive.'

'Don't worry. It's all sorted. They'll edit in the moving scenes. Use a double or something.'

Elliot gets a weird humming near his left ear, as if an insect is buzzing round him. He flaps his hand at it, trying to brush it away. 'I still dunno. It's not what I want.'

'You don't pick and choose on chances like this.' Kris starts pacing the shower room. 'It's exposure you need. As much as we can pull together. It's taken a lot of time setting this up.'

Elliot flaps at his ear again. He doesn't want cars and adverts. He wants to be about words and music. 'I need some time to think this through.'

Kris stops pacing and faces Elliot, shaking his head. 'You've got to shape up a bit. I know everything's looking great, but we need to seize the moment. It's easier to slip out of the limelight than it is to get in. And once you're out . . .'

'Just—give me a bit of space.'

'There isn't time. They've got a deadline and they'll hook up with someone else if we don't give them an answer.'

Elliot's eyes meet Kris's. 'It just—it feels wrong.

Like it's not really me.'

'No publicity is wrong. Not if it gets your face seen and your name known.'

'We're doing all right, aren't we?'

'Look—you don't know this business like I do. You have to grab at everything. You don't make money out of the music on its own any more. I mean—come on—even your ringtone has earned you more than your single.'

The insect in Elliot's left ear drones louder. He rubs at it. Scratches. Images zap through his head. Crowds swaying. Hands reaching up to him. A 'We Love You Elliot' banner. He hears his voice saying, 'I don't care about the money.'

Kris seems to turn to him in slow motion. His face locks into a tight, almost pained expression, like a runner taking on one lap too many. Then something in him seems to flip. His eyes blaze, and anger spins from him. '*You* don't care. *You* don't care. How the hell do you think I can keep this machine running with a stuffed-up attitude like that. Travelling. Equipment. Dancers. Roadies. I'm not your effing father. I'm not doing all this for . . .'

He stops then, but his eyes still burn.

Elliot battles against the insect drone. It is crawling across his brain. 'Finish it,' he says quietly. 'Finish what you were going to say.'

Kris shakes his head, his jaw set. 'It doesn't matter.'

The silence between them is a loaded gun.

Kris sighs suddenly. Glances at his watch. 'Look—

you get yourself dressed. We've got to get moving. I'll meet you by the main door, and we'll talk about this again later.'

Elliot watches him go. He pulls on his shirt and fumbles with the buttons, the blisters stinging from the cream. He's cold now. Shivering. He knows the word that Kris was missing. It's missing from a lot of things. Too many things.

Love.

And then he thinks about Anna. Once his name is really fixed—once Kris is confident they've got enough behind them—maybe Elliot will stand more of a chance with being honest about her. Maybe he'll have more of a voice, and Kris will ease up on him a bit.

But he's not there yet. He's got to toughen up. Roughen up. It's easier to slip out of the limelight than it is to get in. He puts his jacket on, slings his bag over his shoulder, and heads out to the foyer. Kris has his back to Elliot, and is watching a white limousine slide up alongside the marble steps.

The shimmery bikini girls are out in the foyer too, sitting in an alcove drinking more cocktails, draped around Jack and Ryan. They don't look round as Elliot walks by.

Kris turns as he approaches, shooting him a brief smile. 'The car's here.'

'That ad,' says Elliot. 'It'll be OK. I'll do it.'

Kris touches his shoulder. Nods. Grins. 'Good,' he says. 'Just trust me. I know what I'm doing, and it's for the best. Everything I do for you is for the best. And just to show I care about you—and to prove I want you to get positive experiences from everything that's going on, I've set something up for you. A sort of gift.'

'Yeah?'

'It's a visit. To the country.'

Elliot frowns. It sounds like a picnic by a stream.

'To see someone you know—or at least someone you might think would be worth knowing.'

'What you on about?'

'I've booked you a meeting with Marc Wild. You're going to spend an evening over at The House. It's been a nightmare trying to pull it together, but I've just tied it up with Hal Brent—his manager—now. Friday the third of June. Don't worry—you're free—I've checked.'

Pressed tight in the Corner,
tried to grip the wall.
Stars burn out to nothing
as they fall.

Elliot—photos and links offered by hardsell.com

hardsell.com has links to the best Elliot Heath photos and posters . . . 'Hands Off' Untouchable tour T-shirts/hats and other merchandise available.
Home>E>Elliot.com . . .
http://www.hardsell.com/c04/Elliot-Heathhtml

Chapter Thirty-Six

'We can do it on the Sunday. It's only two days later.' Elliot scratches Boris's ears, and Boris whimpers and edges closer to the chair, his scruffed head resting on Elliot's knee.

'You promised *that* day. My birthday. It was going to be special.' Anna's back is rigid as she stands at the cooker, stirring some rice concoction her mum had left for them before she'd gone off to the stables.

'D'you think I should've turned it down?' Guilt stiffens his voice.

'Yes.' She stirs faster, splats of pepper and mushroom spilling over the side of the pan, spitting in the flame.

Elliot takes in the way her hair tumbles down over her shoulders. She hadn't been expecting him—he's fitted her in with a visit to Dad again—and she's in old paint-smeared jeans and a sloppy beige top. She looks great.

Boris shuffles closer and offers Elliot his paw. Elliot takes it, shakes it, then places it firmly on the floor. 'I came today because I wanted to tell you to your face. Not just with a text, or anything like that.'

'How very thoughtful of you.'

The insect drone starts up in his head again. 'This invitation is pretty important. To me.'

'It's *all* important to you.' She adds a fierce sprinkling of paprika to the mix.

'It's just that—he's the closest thing to who *I* want to be, one day.'

'I'm always last on your list of things to do. I don't matter.'

'Of course you matter.' He razors his fingers through his hair. She is glaring round at him now. Elliot thinks he can smell burning, but this probably isn't the time to say. Boris slinks away under the table.

'If it was anyone else . . . anyone but Marc, I'd have said no. But it's a big chance, Anna—I've got a million and one questions for him. And Kris reckons Marc can help me. He's been where I am. It would be like—I dunno—you getting the chance to meet Picasso or something.'

'He's dead.'

'Well—some other artist. You know what I mean.'

They look away from each other. Anna walks to the drawer and rifles around in it. Elliot feels the warmth of her passing, and wants to grab her. Hold on to her. Make everything be all right.

She picks out a teaspoon and walks back to the cooker again, this time shrinking away from him. Elliot feels the space as fiercely as he felt the warmth.

'Take me with you then,' she says.

'What?'

'Take me.' Her voice is small and defiant. 'To Marc Wild's house.'

'I . . . who would you come as?'

'A bloody Martian. God, I don't know. It's not meant to be fancy dress, is it? Who would you expect me to come as?'

'I'd have to have a reason. Make you my PA or my bodyguard or . . .'

'Don't be stupid.'

'But what can I *do*? Kris knows my every move. He logs it when I fart. How can I slip you in, unnoticed, to a big invite like this.'

She spins to face him, pointing the spoon like a weapon. 'Why couldn't you have told him you were busy that night? Why couldn't you have changed *Marc's* date to Sunday, instead of ours?'

'He's going away. To America. His manager wasn't sure when he was coming back. And Kris said the whole thing was hard enough to set up as it was.'

Anna's eyes are bright with tears. 'I bet you'd bow out of coming to my funeral if you got a better offer.'

'That's a crap thing to say.' Elliot tries to think of an equivalent offer that might happen to her one day. He can't do it. There isn't one. From under the table Boris's tail thumps uncertainly.

Thin black smoke curls up from the pan. The smell of burning has grown stronger. 'I thought you'd understand,' Elliot says helplessly. It sounds lame, but it's partly true. In his more optimistic moments, he'd managed to make himself imagine she might be pleased for him.

She throws the spoon on to the floor, where it pings out a sharp ring of protest. 'You thought I'd understand!' Her voice holds the edge of a shriek. 'That's just it, isn't it? You want me to understand everything about you, but you don't understand anything about me. It doesn't occur to you that there's anything *to* understand from my point of view.'

He stares at her, no words or excuses or explanations in his head. His brain has seized up. 'The rice is burning,' he manages at last.

She fires him one last glare, snatches the pan off the cooker and marches it to the bin, scraping the whole thing into the bag.

'Go and find yourself a takeaway.' She is almost spitting. Elliot can hear the shake in her voice. He still wants to try to make it right. But her next sentence knocks the breath out of him. It is not just his brain that locks—his whole body jolts with the impact. 'I'm beginning to understand what your mum must have gone through with your dad.'

He feels cold. Frozen. There is ice in his veins. How could she say that? How could she use that against him? She is the one person in the world he has ever told—she is the one person in the world he thought was properly on his side.

He stares after her as she swings away, the kitchen door slamming, her feet pounding heavily up the stairs. Boris crawls out from under the table and sits huddled against the door, his eyes willing it to open. He starts up an urgent repetitive whine, his paw scratching at the soft pine.

Elliot gets up and turns off the gas. The flames die with one small tired protest. From upstairs Anna's bed creaks and sighs. He can picture her flung out on it, her face crushed into the pillow. Her hair will spill out round her, wild as a storm. Pulling his mobile from his jacket, he punches out the number for a taxi to take him to Dad's, then walks into the hall. Boris squeezes past him and thunders upstairs, his soft whining plea echoing down from outside her room.

Elliot bangs the front door behind him, then stands in the bus lay-by waiting for the car to come. It has started to rain, a sharp shower that stings his eyes and drums on his face.

He thinks that this time it must really be it. This time he will never see her again.

I froze
against the words
you chose.

Message 1 of 2 Subject 7 of 29
Subject: Elliot
Date: 22/05.18:13 GMT Standard Time
From: Cally787
MsgId: <.00006090@mbs-r02.aol.com>

Has anybody else seen that new singer Elliot? I saw him at Watchford and I absolutely love him and I think he is gorgeous!

Message 1 of 8 Subject 6 of 29
Subject: Elliot
Date: 22/05.18:42 GMT Standard Time
From: Princessprunella
MsgId: 34202.29169.000647@mbs-m05.aol.com>

i just discovered elliot+fink he is great he totlay rocks, is there ne1 who agrees with me ????
if u like him pleze im me!
luv
princess!

Message 6 of 8 Subject 5 of 29
Subject: Elliot
Date: 22/05.23:03 GMT Standard Time
From: Ladybird
Msgld: 09507.00015428@mbs-r06.aol.com>

Yeah Elliot is great!! Did anyone else get to see his Sheffield show?!! I won this great prize and met him beforehand!!! He signed my jeans and took a pic and gave me a hug :-)

Message 7 of 8 Subject 4 of 29
Subject: Re: Elliot
Date: 22/05.23:03 GMT Standard Time
From: Luvchild
Msgld: 05867.37814417@mbs-r06.aol.com>

Missed out on tours. Evry fink sold out. Life sucks!!! But Elliot is grate. A genius. I got Trust Thing last month and thers not a duff song on the hole album.

Can't wait till nxt tour. Nyone no wen its happening?

Chapter Thirty-Seven

Billy Heath hears the scratch of the key in the door. The bash as it opens. The slam as it shuts. Noises, all noises. Why does Elliot have to slam?

Sheba the Second shifts slightly on his lap. She smells warm. Billy likes the warm smell. Elliot didn't believe him about Sheba the Second. Not at first. He thought he'd gone mad and was imagining her. Billy was sorry Elliot had thought that about him. He's not mad. Not going mad.

'Hey, Dad.' Elliot stands in the doorway, looking round, frowning.

Billy looks round with him, trying to see what he's frowning at. There's nothing strange. Just crumpled balls of paper. He'd been trying to write. Trying to write. Always trying to write.

'You OK, Dad?'

Billy squints his eyes. The bash slam is still rolling in his head and it's hard to block it out to let in what Elliot is saying.

'I said—you OK?' Elliot steps nearer, right up close, bends to ruffle Sheba the Second's ears. The edge of his trainer is on one of the crumpled balls.

'I'm trying to write.' Billy keeps one eye on the

crumpled ball. Maybe he should change his mind about that song. Maybe Elliot is squashing the life out of the one song that was going to work. 'I think I'll need that paper you're standing on.'

Elliot stoops to pick it up, smoothing it open.

'No—don't look.' Billy feels a scrambling in his chest. 'Work in progress. Bad luck if it gets seen too soon.'

'Sorry.' Elliot folds the paper carefully, hands it to Billy, and straightens up.

Billy pushes it down the side of the chair cushion, and squints up at Elliot. 'You're so tall,' he says. 'I'd forgotten.' Elliot smells of somewhere else. Touches of fumes and food and people brushing up against him.

'I was only here last week,' says Elliot.

Billy nods and blinks and picks at his sleeve. There's always something—a smudge of something—on his sleeve. Just out of sight. As soon as he goes to pick it off it moves away. As soon as he stops picking, it comes back. One of these days he really *might* go mad, because of that smudge.

'Did you cancel Beverly again? You know I'm paying for her.' Elliot's voice is moody. Teenage boys are moody. Even when they're doing well. Like Elliot. Elliot's doing well.

'You're doing well,' says Billy. 'I'm proud. Makes me proud.' Billy can feel a catch in his throat.

'Dad—I'm trying to help you.'

Billy hears a long sound, a tired sigh, from somewhere near him. What would make that sound?

Maybe a song. One of his other songs, sighing from inside its crumpled ball. The sadness of songs that don't get sung.

'I'll make us some tea.' Elliot's words jerk out round the sigh. He takes his tallness away into the kitchen. Billy can hear the bash bash crashing as he gets the mugs down and fills the kettle. Don't be so noisy. Don't be so noisy.

'Tea sounds good,' he says. 'Thank you.'

Sheba the Second looks up and stares towards the kitchen, then curls asleep again.

Not going mad. Not going mad.

Bash bash crashing.

Billy's ears start buzzing. Loud noises do that. Make the buzzing start. He flaps at his ears. Rubs at them. He has to break the sound molecules up so that they lose their power.

'There you go.' Elliot is beside him, shouting, handing him a mug of tea.

'I need to shave. My head,' says Billy.

One of the songs sighs again.

'Dad—just take your tea. Everything's OK.'

Billy takes it, sips it, letting the burn of it melt the bash bash crashing. Elliot slumps down on to the sofa. His face is all dark as if there is a storm behind it. Teenage boys are moody. Even when they're doing well. 'You're doing well,' he says.

'I need to ask you something.' Elliot startles Billy by leaning forward, really looking into his face. 'It might be hard but—just try.'

Billy squints back. Elliot is tall. Too tall. His legs stretch uncomfortably. He'd forgotten how tall Elliot has grown. Billy thinks he should write a song about tallness. Tall fall scrumpled ball.

Elliot's mouth opens and shuts. 'You and Mum. What actually happened? What made her go?'

The yellow smudge shifts, slides. Billy makes himself ignore it. He can be strong like that. He won't even glance at it. Won't even glance.

'Dad—we've never talked about it. I need to. Now.'

'You're doing well. I'm proud of you.'

'Please, Dad. Please.'

Please. Please.

The words scratch in Billy's head. Elliot used to say that when he was a kid. *Please please, Daddy. Please please.* He would beg for a telly programme. Or a biscuit. Or sometimes a song. Billy fixed him up with an old guitar and they'd strum together, even before Elliot was old enough to go to school. Except Mary couldn't bear it. 'Don't turn him into you. You'll shut me out. You both will. I can't bear it.'

He tried. He really tried. What did she want? Scrabble by the fire?

Watch the flames all leap and roar.

Line your letters.

Triple score.

Billy was no good with shuffling letters about. He liked lyrics. Words flowing and shaping and sharpening up their meanings. Always writing. Always trying to write. There was a day when he grabbed the guitar out of Elliot's hands and waved it at Mary. Pushed it at her. Right here in this front room. 'You learn to bloody play my game. Learn to understand it a bit. Learn to know what I love.'

'I hate it.' She started crying. 'I hate it. Rehearsals. Gigs. You're never here.'

Billy lifted the guitar then, raised it above his head, aimed it at the window.

'No, Daddy. Please. Please.' Elliot was white as chalk. Still and small, his eyes all wide. Not tall then. Not tall at all.

Later she made him make the choice. 'Music or us.' She said it into the darkness of their bedroom.

Billy stared up at the ceiling. He felt it lowering. Lowering. It would squash him. Flatten him. The silence screamed. 'You,' he said at last. 'You and Elliot.'

Mary found his hand beneath the quilt, held it and squeezed. 'Thank you.'

Lowering. Lowering. Billy shakes his head. Shakes the memory out. Elliot. The very tall Elliot. He is staring from the sofa, his mouth opening and shutting.

'Dad? Have you heard anything I've said?'

Billy squints across again. He has a loud buzzing in his ears and it's hard to concentrate. He flaps at it. Rubs at it. Needs to make it go away. 'Never . . . give . . . up . . . your . . . dream.' He speaks slowly, big spaces between each word. The songs in the room start sighing again.

Elliot shakes his head, picks up his tea and swigs

it back. 'I can't stay long,' his opening and shutting mouth says. 'I need to get back to London tonight.'

Billy tries to surprise the yellow smudge with a lurching grab, and fails.

Girl Talk Weekly

Shy about l♥ve

Think all pop stars are insensitive sex maniacs? The 'Untouchable Elliot' talks to Adele Keight about love, ambition, and the virtues of being a single lad.

The stereotype of hard living, hard loving pop stars may be the one the papers like to push, but our 'Boy of the Week' reveals how his work is more important to him than any sort of love life.

The subject of your love life has become almost a national pastime. Can a hunky, hot-blooded male in his teens really have the self discipline to 'hold back' from all those steamy offers?
I wouldn't ever go for a one-nighter. I'd want to spend some time with the girl. Get to know her properly. But at the moment I'm so taken up with performing, I guess there isn't a lot of space left over for romance.

So what do you do to chill out?
Most spare time is spent writing. Scribbling down ideas and lyrics. Obviously I'll listen to music—any music really. I used to hang out at other gigs, but that's gone a bit crazy since I started getting recognized.

So—our final question—if someone fantastic did come on to you one night, how would you turn her down without hurting her feelings?
Just by being honest. I'm 100 per cent convinced that a girlfriend would be wrong for me at the moment.

Well, that's it, girls. And it's hard to believe, but we think he means it. Unless, of course, you're that one in a million girl who can make him change his mind . . .

Chapter Thirty-Eight

The limousine rolls slowly through the village. 'Somewhere near here.' Elliot squints out through the tinted window, the flint grey cottages smudged together in the dusk. 'It's supposed to be up a turning past the pub.'

A minute later they are bumping up a potholed drive, the strange spindled house that is Marc Wild's appearing, then disappearing, through the gaps in the trees. Elliot can feel this moment in his spine.

He had a poster with The House in the background—it hung in his room when he was about ten. Marc Wild stands in a shimmery blue garden, a giant moon rising up from behind a wintered tree. The poster came with a CD called 'Being Different'. Mum took it down, threatening to do a 'decorating' stint. She never did. The shape of the poster is still there, a ghosted rectangle on the wall.

They crunch to a halt and Elliot climbs out, walking slowly, drinking in the scene. Close up, The House seems draped in neglected grace, a silver-haired old lady in moth-eaten silks. Arched, latticed windows stare out at the evening, as if they are waiting for carriages that never come. Some of the panes are cracked. The tower leans awkwardly from the oddly pitched roof. A strong wind—a storm wind—might blow the whole place away.

There are two cars parked near the porch, an ink-blue Range Rover and a silver Rolls Royce. Further along, beneath the tower, is an ancient bus. Elliot can see ivy tracing the edges of the passenger windows, looking for a way in.

There are no lights anywhere.

Behind him the chauffeur walks over, the crunch of his footsteps filling the quiet. 'This doesn't seem like a place expecting guests, sir.'

Elliot feels an edge of panic. The last few days have fizzed him up—just the thought of coming here. What if Kris got it wrong? The address—or even the invitation? He couldn't bear the empty drive back home to London. And he'll have blown out Anna for nothing. 'There must be people here—there's cars and everything. And it's all been set up. Kris doesn't usually mess up on arrangements.'

'It's a sprawling great place, sir, maybe they're in a different bit of the building.' The chauffeur's voice is reassuring. 'Do you want me to check round the side?'

'Hang on—I'll try here first.' Elliot steps past the vine-laced porch posts and knocks on the door.

Flakes of paint dust down onto the mossy tiles.

Nothing happens.

He knocks again.

This time, from somewhere at the back of the house, a light comes on. A moment later the door winces open and a girl looks at him through black oriental eyes.

'I help you?'

'I'm Elliot. Elliot Heath.'

'Who?'

'I'm supposed to see Marc Wild. This is the right place?'

'Who asked you come?'

'His manager.' Elliot chases his memory. 'Hal Brent.'

She shrugs. 'Hal's out at moment but—' She shrugs again, then nods. 'OK. Follow, please.'

Elliot turns and nods at the driver. 'Reckon it's OK now,' he says. 'Thanks for bringing me.'

'Very good, sir.' The driver nods, then goes back to the limousine, the engine starting with a smooth hum as Elliot steps forward to follow the black-eyed girl.

The musty hall has a collection of pop icon photographs skewed along the walls. John Lennon. Mick Jagger. Dylan. Jimmi Hendrix. Marc is there, too, mostly from the old days. Elliot thinks that you could tell just from Marc's eyes that he's 'someone'. No one with eyes like that could have stayed in the shadows.

Elliot keeps walking. Keeps following. They turn a corner and light shudders out from behind a half opened door. There are voices inside the room. Hoots and shouts and bursts of laughter.

Elliot gets the sudden need to hang on to the girl's arm. 'What's your name?' For once, he needs to be talking. To linger.

'Mei Ying.' She gives him a thin, tight smile that tells him she doesn't do small talk. 'Go through. They been going a while.'

Elliot pushes at the door. Going where?

Three blokes sprawl across a faded Persian rug, lying sideways on to Elliot. They don't look round; instead their gaze stays fixed on silent black-and-white images that fuzz out from a giant TV screen.

Only a mangy grey lurcher, curled at the end of a dusty green chaise longue, steadies a look Elliot's way.

Elliot's own eyes rest on Marc, trying to ignore the thinning hair on the back of his head. He used to write letters to Marc, a scrawl of earnest questions about lyrics and chords and what backing worked best with what effect. He never sent them, but somehow just writing them helped him work out the answers for himself. How many songs has this genius helped him with? How many days has he got Elliot through?

The girl on the TV, soft-faced and young, is miming her scene to a devil-haired man.

One of Marc's mates begins dubbing her words, throwing back his head, 'Henry—oh, Henry. Surely you cannot mean these things.' His voice is mocking and high. A pantomime dame. Marc and his other mate hoot and shout, their shoulders shaking.

Elliot's eyes slide to a small coffee table with a carved box in the centre. There are three rolled ten pound notes laid out beside the box, and a gold credit card propped against the lid.

On the screen the devil-haired actor's face twists with tortured despair. Marc dubs this part, his tone manfully deep. 'But, Amelia, I am only thinking of what is best for you, my dear.'

Both mates howl, curling up and rocking.

Elliot shifts uncomfortably. The only OK thing about this scene is the stack of instruments over by the fireplace. A couple of Wildcat guitars. An antique mandolin. A muddle of speakers and a Yamaha amp, half covered by a rich green rug.

Mei Ying picks her way between the three blokes, touches Marc on the shoulder. 'You have guest.'

Marc looks up, looks round, then scrambles to his feet. He is, of course, smaller than Elliot had expected.

'A guest.' He grins. Holds out his hand. His eyes, close up, are bloodshot.

'I'm Elliot. Elliot Heath. Our managers set this up. But if it's a bad time . . .'

'Bad time?' Marc glances down at the other two, who are still doubled up in front of the black-and-white film. 'No, it's not a bad time. It's a great time. We're having a great time. Join us.' He splutters suddenly, like a schoolboy who's just put a toad on the teacher's chair, then bends and takes one of the rolled-up notes, snorting up out of the box. A small cloud of white powder dusts down on to the table.

Elliot wonders if anyone would stop him if he just turned round and went.

Mei Ying watches Marc for a moment. 'You must ask Elliot Heath sit down.'

Marc sucks in his cheeks, chewing at the inside of his mouth. 'That'll be good. Sitting is good.' He speaks fast and low now, his fingers drumming against his leg. He doesn't ask Elliot sit down.

Elliot wonders how far away the limousine is. He can call the chauffeur on his mobile, and wait outside for him. Or he could walk to that pub. It will be better to wait in the pub.

He glances at Mei Ying, who is still watching Marc. 'I think . . .'

The lurcher barks twice, then jumps down from the chaise longue, leaping past everyone.

'Hey—easy, Jackson.'

'Watch it.'

'Go steady.'

Jackson bounds on, past Elliot and towards the door.

Elliot turns as a tall, trim guy walks into the room. 'Oh, son, I'm so sorry. I'm Hal. Marc's manager. I've been held up in London. I'd wanted to be here before you.' He grips Elliot's hand. 'Welcome to The House. I'm glad you could make it. It might've been a bit of time before we were back this way again. So—how you getting on with Kris? We know each other from way back.' He doesn't wait for an answer, but turns to Marc. 'Elliot's the kid who's done the "Untouchable" single. Remember the one I downloaded for you last night?'

Marc nods his head in fast, jerking movements, but his eyes are blank.

'We loved it.' Hal looks back at Elliot. 'It had touches of Marc. Something he might have done himself.'

Marc switches a look round to Hal. 'My sort of song?'

'Your sort of song.'

The bloodshot eyes swim in on Elliot now. 'What's your song called again?'

'"Untouchable".'

'Someone write it for you?'

'No.' Elliot can see the shapes behind Marc's questions, and wishes he could give different answers. *Yes, someone wrote it for me. No, I could never write anything that comes anywhere close. Don't worry about me. I'm not important. Not a threat.*

Marc looks as if the carpet beneath him is beginning to heave. 'Is it doing well?'

Elliot glances at Hal, who is letting Jackson chew his fingers. 'It's OK, I s'pose.'

Marc is shaking now. 'The business is all crap at the moment. Gone wrong. Half the kids in the charts can't even sing. Can you sing?'

Elliot's mind clutches at answers, his own ground moving. 'Not like you could,' he says at last.

'Could?' Marc's head jerks again.

'Come on.' Hal is suddenly there, his hand on Marc's shoulder. 'Give the kid a break. He's come to meet you. You inspire him. Inspire lots of them.'

'Could. Did.'

'Still do,' Elliot interrupts. 'You still inspire me.'

Marc's eyes search Elliot's face, and then something new seems to switch in him, and he starts to grin. The grin stretches to a laugh. He guffs and giggles, shooting looks over his shoulder. 'Hey, you two. Douggie. George. Meet this new noise. Elliot Hive.'

Pantomime dame bloke scrabbles up. 'Sorry, pal—we're not ignoring you—just got caught up in the moment. George—get up, you rude git. This is—sorry—who did you say you were?'

'Elliot.'

George switches off the screen. 'Hey, man. Good to see ya. Goin' all right?' He is chewing gum, his pupils bright pinpricks of light.

It suddenly clicks with Elliot who they are. Douggie Drummond and Georgie Frampton. Both major backing musicians for Marc.

'Fancy a line, pal?' Douggie nods towards the rolled up notes.

'I . . .'

'It's good stuff.' George grins. Chews. Nods his head. 'Man—you'll be singing on the ceiling.'

Elliot glances at Hal, who reads the look. 'I'll get you a drink.' He heads across the room to the drinks cabinet, holding up a bottle and calling, 'This vodka do you?'

Elliot doesn't want vodka either, but he has to go along with something. 'Thanks.'

Hal pours himself one, too, then steers Elliot to a lumpy chair in the corner. 'Dump yourself here. Get used to the scene a bit. Marc doesn't mean to offend—he's just a bit wired tonight.'

Elliot lets himself settle, aware of the others snorting coke, trying not to watch. They all talk, but nobody says anything real. Jokes. Banter. Something about a shot away gig in France last year.

Mei Ying doesn't take part. Not even with the vodka. She curls on the floor next to Marc, her head on his shoulder, staring through the long arched window into the night.

Elliot thinks that Anna sat with him like that. Once upon a time.

He wonders what she's doing now. He wonders if she's out celebrating her birthday. And he wonders who she's celebrating it with. He swigs suddenly at the vodka. The heat of it is a cold flame in the centre of him. Like something living. Outside, the moon pours silver. Stars glitter in. It's not so bad. He's here, with Marc Wild. Being different.

Douggie reaches for a Wildcat and begins strumming, the sound moving through the room like something living.

Elliot closes his eyes. He used to dream of a time like this. He knocks back more vodka. Hal fills his glass again. Then again. Marc is singing now and Elliot thinks that whatever happened to his eyes hasn't happened to his voice.

He'd like to sing too, but he doesn't want to risk it. Marc seems OK about him being here now. That's good enough for him. So instead he stares up at the ornate moulded ceiling, blanketed by the moment. He can't work out what he is feeling. His cheeks seem wet.

Somewhere through it all he gets a vague idea that he needs the bathroom. He thinks he asks where it is. He thinks someone tells him. When he stands up the door is a moon distance away. The room lurches as he walks.

'He'll feel like crap tomorrow,' someone says.

Elliot hears it, but he's not certain who the speaker means.

Spin the bottle just once more.
Watch the genie spill out on the floor.

Chapter Thirty-Nine

Elliot is shivering, slumped in the bath. He's not sure where his clothes are, and he gets the vague idea that he ought to care, but doesn't. Mei Ying is sluicing him down, water raining out from a shower-head. He ought to care about that too, but she is brisk and efficient and she's got the air of someone who's coping. Coping seems as if it's probably a good thing. He needs her to cope. He thinks the raining out water is probably too cold, but his head hammers and it's all too hard to think about.

He tries to straighten up, fixing a stare on the coloured tiles, but the shine of them slides inside his eyes. Under his lids. It presses. It pushes.

Mei Ying moves round behind him. 'The alcohol has poisoned you. I do this now so cool you down. Otherwise blood in you will boil. It will boil and boil and cook your brain.' Her voice is dispassionate. The voice of someone who has done this too many times before. Elliot puts his hand to his face and his skin is crawling hot. Maybe his brain is bubbling up already. The cells molten liquid. Steam in his ears.

'It is good thing I find you. You sick. Very sick. All over floor.'

He swallows, and his throat stings with the

scrawned, burnt feeling that tells him it's true. Sick. Very sick. He glances sideways at the floor, which has damp towels and flannels laid out over it.

'Sorry. Thanks.' He tries to straighten up, and his melted brain slops round inside his skull. 'I'll do this. You don't have . . .'

'Stay still.' Her voice is a command. He has to trust her. Boiling blood is not a good thing.

'Hal has not looked after you.' She rests one hand on his shoulder, tilting him forward. 'He put you on scrappy tip with Marc if you not watchful.'

'Yeah.' Elliot hasn't a clue what she's talking about, but he will agree with her about anything.

'Hal get you come The House to wake Marc up. Change his way. The competition you bringing. You all very hungry for big prize, I think.'

'Yeah.'

'Hal think you next King of Music. This Marc's crown. He hope Marc will not want you to snatch crown away.'

'Yeah. I mean no. That's not it. Not what I was wanting.' This is too many words for Elliot. He closes his eyes. He is spinning.

'You—maybe no. But Hal—he keeps eye on best chance. Forget how to watch for sunset. They all drive me screwy. They boys in men's bodies. Killing themselves. Now Marc have to go to America for detox. So much money. All talent waste.'

Elliot opens his eyes to look at her. She is saying something he ought to be listening to, but her face keeps slipping in and out of focus and her words slide away. He pictures them falling out of her mouth, dissolving in the swirl of water.

'Come on.' She turns the shower off, and the graunching sound of the taps makes him wince. As she helps him to stand she pulls a towel down from the rack, laying it gently round his shoulders. Then she leads him from the room as if he too is just another boy. 'I put you in bed.'

When he wakes, he has no idea of the time. He edges himself upright gingerly, shivering and pulling the patchwork quilt right up to his chin. There are green and yellow patterns on the quilt. Too much colour. Too much tiny fantastic detail. His eyes ache. His throat hurts.

Someone has put a glass of water on the table next to the bed, but the effort of stretching his hand out to lift it feels huge, and he gives up. His mobile is there too. Someone's been taking care of him. He has a vague memory of Mei Ying, and the bathroom, but the images seem patchy. Manic patterns on a quilt. He can't make them into a proper picture.

Outside, there are birds singing. A thin light pierces a gap in the faded velvet curtains. Elliot can't bear the thought of the day outside.

Never again.

But just now, he has to sleep. His eyelids weigh down, the darkness drawing him. Sinking. Sinking.

When his mobile goes off he jolts, panicked, and nearly knocks over the glass, although he's pretty sure it must be Kris. He'd got him to change his number last week—he reckoned he was getting too many time-wasting calls—and now hardly anyone knows it but Kris.

'Elliot?'

'Yeah?' He steadies the water, holding the mobile slightly away from his ear. He wants to tell Kris not to shout.

'I've been trying you for ages. How'd it go last night?'

Elliot hesitates. 'Different.' Being different. A line seems to run from that worshipped CD to here.

'Glad you went?'

Elliot hesitates again. 'Not sure yet. Need some time to think it through.'

'I wanted you to see it. A bit of a warning.'

'What d'you mean?' Elliot wants to sleep again. Sleep sleep sleep for a hundred years.

'All the drugs. And the drink. Marc was a miracle find when he started out. I just want you to know the dangers.'

So it wasn't a gift, after all. It was a lesson. 'Basic psychology?' Elliot isn't sure whether he feels grateful, or used.

'You could say. But for your own good. It's all for your good. Now listen—I've got some fantastic news.'

'Yeah?' Has he learnt Kris's lesson? He'll never do drugs anyway—not after seeing what even legal ones have done to Dad—and the drinking was a one off. The whole evening was a one off.

'It's a gig. A big one. The Obelisk charity event in Hyde Park at the end of the month. Bobby Lewis has pulled out, and they've shuffled the acts round. Found a place for you.'

'Yeah?' Elliot reaches for the water and it turns his stomach as he sips.

'Wait till you hear the line-up. They've got Heaven Scent, Sabotage . . .' Kris reels out a list, a tumble of names bumping and thumping.

Elliot sinks back on the pillow.

'. . . Josh Steine pushed to get you in there. I hardly had to do a thing. It's all coming together. Really moving.'

The House all round him seems very quiet. Everything sleeping.

'. . . So I've ordered you a car—I gather from Hal you stayed at The House . . .'

'Yeah.' Elliot tries to picture Marc in a bed somewhere near him. Or maybe he just passed out in the room downstairs. Could he really end up like that?

'. . . the car will bring you straight to the studio. We need to get to work on a top set for this. Obelisk are pushing for a new album if it all goes well. Elliot? You still there?'

'Yeah. Thanks.'

'See you soon.' The call ends.

Elliot closes his eyes, still too washed-out to think about new gigs. Even at Hyde Park. He understands what Kris was trying to do with his lesson. And why. But he's not sure if it makes sense to him.

Marc is a mess. He can see that. But Marc followed his dream—had everything he could ever have wanted. How can something so right, go wrong? So maybe there aren't any answers. Whatever happens must happen. In the end, there's no choice.

He misses Anna. Aches for her. He even sort of understands what she meant—that thing she came out with about Mum and Dad. It was hard to hear it, but in a way, there was a future looming where they might have headed down that road. He suddenly wishes he could tell her. What if something bad happened to him—what if he died—and she didn't know he had thought it through? She could live out her whole life not knowing how he'd felt.

Outside, there are still birds singing. And suddenly it seems that the patterns have made a clear picture at last. Shifting himself up on to one elbow, he reaches for his mobile again. Punches in Anna's number. She'll probably at least answer, because she won't know who it is at first. Even if she screams and swears and tells him to get stuffed, it will be worth it just to have made contact.

Would you talk to a kick in the head like me?
Took a wake-up call
to shake my senses free.

WEBPOP NEWS

Elliot is the one to watch. His single **'Untouchable'** is already the fastest chart climber this year, and his DVD sales have pushed him past the phenomenal record set by Traci Maran — last year's 'Big Thing'. Shame to see her sliding so soon.

So . . . a **big thank you** to everyone who came to Elliot's tour this spring and made the shows what they were, and to all of you who have bought the single and DVD!!!

CLICK HERE to check out August **LIVE GIG DATES** with the **UNTOUCHABLE ELLIOT**

Chapter Forty

Beverly helped Billy stick post-it notes all round the house when he told her Elliot was on telly, to help him remember the time and the channel. She's good to him, Beverly. Now that she's learnt not to throw his songs away. But he didn't need the notes. Didn't need reminding.

He's been up since dawn, playing with the switches, checking that the telly works. Turning it off. Turning it on. Turning it off. Turning it on. What if there's a power cut? What if a mouse bites through the cable? But he's got a cat. He won't have mice if he's got a cat. Won't have mice if he's got a cat.

He sits back in the chair and taps a beat out on his knee.

Won't get mice if you've got a cat.

Won't get lice if you wear a hat.

Clean the teeth of your vampire bat.

Won't get mice if you've got a cat.

He stands up and checks the switch again. Turning it off. Turning it on. What if the batteries die in the remote?

What if you lose the oars on your boat?

Won't get mice if you've got a cat.

* * *

Sheldon edges the Saab towards the festival car park, and Mary opens the window, letting the air breeze in. She and Billy brought Elliot here as a child. It was a heatwave then too. He knelt on the grass and tried to make friends with a mangy looking pigeon with a broken wing. There must be a photo somewhere. She'd tried to get Billy in it, too, but he got talking to a busker and they had some great debate about second-hand guitars. Typical Billy. It wasn't the music that had driven her mad. It was the way it shut her out.

And now she is going round again. Elliot. Elliot. The posters are everywhere. They have a sticker on the car and a programme of the day.

When she'd rung him, Elliot insisted he could get them in free, but she refused.

'We'll pay our way. It's a charity do, after all,' she said.

She looks up at the sky, where a silver balloon floats higher and higher, drifting away.

'There's a lot of people going in,' says Sheldon, resting one hand on the steering wheel, and the other one on her leg. 'It'll be busy.'

She nods. 'And hot for Elliot. Under the lights.' She thinks of things like this now.

How it must feel. What an audience must look like from the stage. How tired he must get. Sometimes she tries to ask him, but he just shrugs. Keeps her shut out. He will never quite forgive her for leaving him. She will never quite forgive herself. She thinks of Billy, who still doesn't go out of the house. Who hasn't got it in him to come and see his son live the dream he never managed to live for himself.

Why had they had to fall in love with each other? He'd have been so much happier with someone else. And she wouldn't have had to carry the weight of what he'd given up to please her. Except Elliot is up there now—doing what Billy wanted. And doing it better. If it hadn't been for her and Billy, there wouldn't have been Elliot. She wishes she could tell Elliot how proud she is, but she knows he'd only throw the words back at her. Bruise her with the past. She got it wrong—with both of them. Tried to tie them down. But she'd been scared. Scared about money. Scared about the future if Billy didn't make it. Scared about Elliot making all the same mistakes. And if she's honest, she was angry too. Angry that Billy was out doing everything he wanted, while she was at home keeping everything ticking for when he came back.

Her own mum had put up with a life like that, her dad chasing acting parts all over the country, and she'd been determined—even desperate—not to repeat that pattern again.

'You OK?' Sheldon's hand finds hers. Squeezes it. Sheldon with his safe computer company world. Sheldon who always puts her first.

She nods, leans forward, pulls a tissue from the box on the dashboard and blots the silent tears from her cheeks. 'Just a bit hot, that's all.'

The car bumps through into the parking field; a

nose-studded girl in raggy jeans points them to a space. Mary wonders if the girl's mum battled with her about the nose stud.

As they walk through the gate, just near the entrance, a thin-faced boy with an earring is selling balloons blazoned with the names of bands. 'Look at that,' whistles Sheldon, giving Mary a nudge, 'The silver ones have got "ELLIOT" on them.'

Anna stands pressed up against the front of the stage, the string of her silver *Elliot* balloon wound tightly round her wrist. She'll keep the balloon for ever, even when it's gone down, along with all the postcards he's started sending her. Special messages. Snatches of songs and poems. Showing how he feels with his words.

She's lost Lucy—she's gone off to scream at The Sessions on the next stage, but she knows where she is. And anyway, she'll see the balloon. Anna's been in this spot all day, terrified that if she wanders off she might lose her place at the front.

The last band who were on—Skunk Fudge—are wrapping down their gear, and Elliot's crew are hurrying his on. There's a backdrop—a collage of HANDS OFF signs, padlocks, and barbed wire. A giant glass prism is wheeled on to the centre of the stage.

She feels tingly seeing Elliot's name running across the sides of the equipment. She wishes she could tell someone she knows him. She's with him. But it's enough, for the moment, that they're back together. She's got to learn to put up with the life. And the secrets. As long as she trusts him, it'll work.

More people are gathering. 'What's he like?' A bloke with a scraggy beard and red bandana peers uncertainly at the stage.

'God—what rock have you been hiding under? He's amazing. The next big thing. Everyone says so.' The girl with him pins her stream of raven hair back from her face and hustles in next to Anna, knocking against the string. The balloon dances madly, as if the music has already started.

Anna and Raven Hair nod at each other. Grin. All fans together. Friends for the day. Anna thinks it's a great feeling. Warming.

'Have you seen him before?' Raven Hair turns her back on Bandana Boy, as if she's too disgusted even to look at him.

'A few times.' Anna's voice is thick with secrets that Raven Hair mustn't guess. 'Have you?'

Raven Hair nods. 'Whenever I can. I follow him around. I reckon he's *gorgeous*. Don't you?'

'Yes.' Anna blocks out the tiny sting of insecurity prickling at her. Raven Hair won't ever get anywhere near him. And even if she did, he wouldn't be interested. She's got to remember that. Put up with the life. A sort of trust thing. She'll say that to herself, like a mantra, every time it starts to worry her.

It's still ages to go before he's on.

Raven Hair settles on the grass with Bandana Boy,

curling against him. He's obviously been forgiven. Anna gets the feeling they haven't known each other very long. Probably they've only just met.

Her legs are aching, and it feels mad to keep standing, so she sits down too, tilting her face up and letting the sun pour down on her. It's sticky hot and she's sweating in the 'Hands Off' T-shirt. When Lucy comes back, she'll leave her to guard the spot and go and get an ice cream.

Muffled music thrums out across the field. A loudspeaker announces something that Anna can't work out, but it doesn't matter. It's a long way away. Like something in a dream.

A woman comes over and crouches down beside her, flashing a smile. 'Hi.'

'Hi.'

'I'm a reporter, I work freelance,' she says, handing Anna a card. 'Here to do a review of the day. Can I ask you a few questions about what you've seen so far?'

Anna glances at the card but doesn't read it. She's been handed all sorts of leaflets and freebies since she's been here, and this card will end up in the grass, like the rest of them. She won't do it yet though. She couldn't be rude like that. 'I haven't seen anything. I'm only waiting for Elliot.'

The reporter pulls out a notebook. 'So you're a big fan, are you? What is it you like about him?'

'I . . .' Anna hesitates. She has to be careful. The last thing she wants is her picture taken, and for someone to see them out somewhere together later, and to put the two together. 'Try that girl there—the one with the long black hair. She knows loads more about him than I do.'

The reporter flashes out the smile again. 'Thanks—but give me a call if you fancy a bit of fame. I might run something on Elliot fans. You could get your name in the paper.' She edges away from Anna, talks to Raven Hair, handing out another card and scribbling spidery black notes in her book.

'One two. One two.' The sound guys are running the test. More people shuffle through, the audience growing. The reporter woman moves on. Anna sees her accost another girl. Pale skin and stunning burn-red hair. She looks familiar. Maybe she's famous—a model or something. Surely, if Elliot knew that someone like *that* was following him around, he might be tempted. Any bloke would. Anna pulls herself back to the moment and makes herself stand up, realizing Lucy won't be able to see the balloon if she's sitting down.

Raven Hair and Bandana Boy stand up too. Anna won't let herself look at Stunning Red-Head again. The mood around the stage has changed. There's a sense of things closing in. Tightening.

A group next to Anna—all about her age—struggle out of their tops and switch into the Hands Off T-shirts that are being sold over near the beer tent. Lots of them have bought the caps too. Anna digs the one Elliot sent her out of her bag, the black denim peak a welcome shade in the heat.

The sound crew have left the stage. The equipment looks set.

The crowd presses in on her. She hadn't realized it had got so packed. There's no way she'll get through to buy an ice cream, and Lucy won't be able to pick out her balloon. There's hundreds of them here now, all bobbing and blowing, the sun flashing on the silver.

The backing band is already coming on.

Any minute now . . . Any minute now . . .

'I thought I was going to miss it.' Lucy squeezes in next to Anna's shoulder. The Sessions did three encores. I couldn't tear myself away . . . Oh hey—look—they're blowing coloured smoke all round that pyramid—I think it's about to happen!'

'How did you . . .' Anna starts, but she doesn't finish.

Billy pulls his chair closer to the screen. Sheba the Second is warm in his lap. He leans forward and turns the sound up. Everything's working. Won't get mice if you've got a cat.

The camera is showing the crowd. The idea of being squashed against people makes him shrink back into the cushion. But he must watch. Must watch. Must watch.

The backdrop to the stage is a mess of writing. Billy squints but his eyes aren't what they were. He can't make it out. A giant glass prism beams rainbows out from its sides. Rainbows.

Dreams.

Never give up your dreams.

And then suddenly the squashed together people seem to surge forward, there is a roar, clouds of rainbow colour smoking up from the stage.

And then Elliot is up there like a god amongst the coloured clouds, and the squashed together people hold their hands out to him as if he is someone who will save them. Billy is proud. So proud.

His son out there. His boy. His little boy. He could always sing—right from a baby. Billy remembers practising in the front room—this same front room—and Elliot in a soft blue chair that Mary used to strap him in suddenly cooing out a string of sounds in tune. Perfect pitch. Not words, but sounds. He learnt to sing before he could talk. How normal is that?

He wishes Beverly was here. So he could say to her, 'That's Elliot. That's him there.' He says it to Sheba the Second. 'That's Elliot. That's him there.' He tries to shift her position so she is facing the screen, but she stiffens and jumps down from him. Taking her warmth away.

'That's Elliot. That's him there.' Billy says it again, to nobody now. His hands have started to shake.

And suddenly the thought screams through him that he should be there, sharing all this with Elliot. He knows the music business. He should be watching from the side, humping gear, checking everything's OK. Being there for when Elliot comes off. You need someone for when you come off—someone to wind down with. Someone to keep you out of trouble.

He'd wanted that from Mary, and never got it. The least he could have done was give it to his son.

Billy realizes his cheeks are wet. His eyes running. His nose running. He wants to change. He wants to put things right. He stretches his shaking hands out towards the screen.

Save me, Elliot. Save me.

From the back of the crowd Mary is aware of a surging forward. A cheer. A roar. And on the giant screens at either side of the stage there is Elliot. Two Elliot's. Each image hazed behind a fog of colour.

'Can you see all right? Shall we move closer?' Sheldon is nudging her like a schoolboy offering toffees.

She doesn't answer. She can't answer. She stands frozen in the blazing day, her arms hugged tight around her chest, her face twisting as she tries to block the tears.

Elliot. Her Elliot. And all these youngsters screaming and calling out his name. She's done a lot wrong. If she could turn back time there's so much she would change.

But looking at him now—so talented, so handsome, so confident as he moves out from the mist—she knows that amongst all the mess that makes the past, she's still been part of something that was good.

There's a sea of sound—a surge from the crowd—and Anna is pressed forward as Elliot appears, stepping out of the prism, singing. Golden and gorgeous. Bigger than everyone. Than everything. Is this Elliot? Her Elliot? Anna doesn't know whether to stare at him, or at the close-up image on the video screen. She feels sick. Knocked away. And stupidly—shy. He's part god up there. A beautiful stranger.

Glancing back over her shoulder, she is staggered by the crush. A thousand balloons now. Banners and flags. We love you, Elliot. We love you. Raven Hair has her arms stretched high in the air, waving and swaying. Bandana Boy is just staring. Mesmerized. A scream goes up as the first song fades away.

The smoke on the stage has thinned, and the giant glass prism is catching the light behind him, throwing out a dazzle of rainbow rays.

'Thank you, everyone. It's fantastic to be here.' His voice. His beautiful voice. Echoey, familiar, and strange.

As she stands, stung by sudden tears, Anna wonders what it must be like up there, looking down on all of this. All these people here for him. And then her hands are stretched out and she is just another mad fan trying to get nearer to the stage.

We love you, Elliot.

We love you.

Knickers skim through the air. Raven Hair hurls some. Tiger striped. Definitely not Aunt Doris Christmas ones. Anna wishes she'd brought her own to throw.

I love you, Elliot. I love you.

Chapter Forty-One

Paige Melder's head throbs as her black Ferrari bumps its way back out of the grassy car park. A girl in torn jeans waves her out through the exit, and Paige edges into the choked evening traffic. She wishes she'd left earlier. It'll take for ever to get through this lot. She's tired and she's sweaty and she hasn't even come out with a decent story. Not anything that a hundred other freelancers won't have got.

God, it's been a rubbish month for stories. And today, there must have been pages-worth of gossip going on behind the scenes, but she couldn't wangle herself near any of it. Security's so tight at these things, and she hadn't managed to get a permit to go backstage.

She stops at a crossing and a straggle of festival goers give her the thumbs up as they pass. They look sunburnt and glowing, and out of their heads. Maybe there's a story there? The danger of decadence at free festivals.

A horn blasts angrily behind her and she realizes the lights have changed. Not that it makes much difference. The traffic is still pretty much at a stand-still. Moving into gear, she is distracted for another moment by a silver helicopter whirring overhead.

One of today's demi-gods, off to that exclusive Obelisk do. God, she'd have killed to get her hands on one of those passes. The most she's managed to do all day is to hand out cards to any kids she thought might look as if they could offer a new angle. Told them to ring her if anything happened.

Not that any of them would. All her swish glossy cards are probably being walked into the ground where they've been dropped. A waste. It's all such a waste. But she'll have to come up with a decent story soon. The next payment on the Ferrari is due in just over a week, and the rent on her apartment is crippling. She'll end up waitressing at this rate.

WELCOME *to the website of*

Elliot

Touch the Untouchable

Click here for live video download!

September tour dates announced
view info >

New single 'Time to Shine' out 4 July
view info >

Join the mailing list here
view info >

2nd Album 'Wake Up Call' out August
view info >

what's new? | back stage | noticeboard | library | members | get stuff | tour info

Chapter Forty-Two

The helicopter tilts sideways, dipping down towards the white-pillared mansion. Elliot presses his forehead against the window, shouting above the noise of the engine, 'It's incredible. Look at it all.'

The high from the gig is still pulsing through him, and the sight of the giant marquee set in the emerald grounds gives him a new rush. They have landed so softly, it takes Elliot a moment to realize they have actually touched down, and he grins round at Kris.

'Feeling OK?' shouts Kris.

'Yeah. Feeling great.'

'Safe to bail out,' calls the pilot.

They make their way to the door.

'Good afternoon, sirs.' A butler in a crisp cream uniform is waiting. 'May I take your bags?'

'No, I'm fine. But thanks.' Elliot can't ever see himself going that far—ever letting anyone fetch and carry for him, and anyway he hasn't got much. His dinner jacket and the rest of his gear for the party were delivered earlier.

Kris hands his own bag across and they follow a crazed path past a glass summer house, through showers of flowers and shiny-leafed shrubs, then climb the stone steps to the mansion's main door.

Inside, their footsteps echo on mosaic tiles, and Elliot walks backwards as he tries to catch all the details of rich bronze sculptures. Fine-legged deer and strangely sculpted hares. Two eyeless greyhounds. A collection of angels. Anna would love all this stuff. He wants to remember it for her.

'Just one room here must cost more than my dad's entire house is worth. How much d'you reckon it would be to run a place like this?'

'A lot of hit singles,' Kris calls back over his shoulder.

'You're telling me.' Elliot catches up with him. 'Still—how much of this could sales from "Untouchable" buy?'

Kris looks round. Shrugs. 'Probably a door.'

Elliot squints at the elaborate doors with their etched glass designs, and shakes his head. 'More like just one of those gold handles,' he says.

'This staircase, sirs.' The butler gestures ahead. 'Your rooms are up here.'

More sculptures. More doors. 'More singles.' Elliot's voice bounces strangely along the vast corridor. He wonders if his room will in any way reflect what he might have earned for Obelisk, but as the butler turns the key and leads him in, he thinks that it probably doesn't.

'Mr Heath's room.'

Elliot walks in. The room drips silver and gold. A

crystal teardrop chandelier hangs from the ceiling. The furniture is draped in silks and velvets, all pastels and patterns.

'Your evening wear is in the wardrobe, sir. And there are buzzers beside all the light switches if you need to call down for service.'

Elliot is bubbling up. He wants to laugh and do cartwheels. Give this butler wild sloppy kisses on the cheek.

'Will that be all for now, sir?'

Elliot wonders if the butler has read his thoughts. 'Yeah. Sorry. Thanks.' But he can't stop turning in slow, amazed circles.

Kris's expression is almost smug. As if the whole place is a parcel he has had prepared, and he is watching Elliot unwrap the layers of paper. 'I'll get off to my room then,' he says suddenly, nodding at the butler. 'I'll buzz you in about an hour. Give you time to get sorted.'

As soon as they have gone Elliot peels off his stale sweaty clothes, exploring the room in his boxer shorts. There's a mini CD player in the corner, and he puts on one of the CDs that are stacked next to it. Heaven Scent kick in—the number they did on *Top of the Pops*. He closes his eyes, his fingers clicking, jiving round the room.

The dance gets wilder. Faster. Grabbing a sequinned silk cushion, he flings it ahead of him, catching it again and pulling it back as if it's a partner. He wishes Anna was here.

As the track ends he bows to the cushion, dropping it back on to the chair. 'Cheers.' He blows it a kiss. 'I'll catch you again later.'

He goes over to a gold cocktail cabinet, pouring himself an iced fruit cocktail. There's vodka in there, but he's not risking that. Never again.

There is a mirror on the wall, crystal-edged and painted with small silver birds. He remembers the cracked scar mirror at The Edge, and the bubbling blows up in him again. He's come a long way, but he's been running blindfold. Not letting himself see ahead. He's got the view in focus now, and it's OK. In fact, it's fantastic. He's on top of the world. The stars. The universe. And if he has his way, he's never coming down.

He texts Anna, even though he knows she'll still be at Hyde Park. The Sessions will be on about now.

Fantastic. Wish u were here. Miss u. x

The bed is in the next room. Huge but intricate, the frame silver, twined with flowers and vines. An exotic magical garden.

He drops the mobile on to a gold embossed table, leaps up on to the green silk duvet, and bounces. If anyone could see him they'd think he'd lost it. But stuff them. Stuff them stuff them stuff them stuff them stuff them. Letting the bounce ebb away, he flops down on to his back and lies staring up at the ceiling.

It is like a picture, the plaster moulded into long-limbed girls half hidden behind intricately patterned leaves. The girls are holding out apples in their smooth slender fingers.

Stretching and sighing, Elliot closes his eyes. The gig is still there, fizzing through him. He's going to take for ever to come down from it.

Still flyin' over heaven—
view is pretty clear.
Whole place ripe with paradise.
Wishin' you were here.

Chapter Forty-Three

It's his mobile going off that wakes him.

'Elliot?'

It's Kris.

'Yeah?' His head feels muzzy. He hadn't meant to sleep.

'You nearly sorted? Only we ought to get down there soon. I don't want everyone to be too out of it to remember the intros.'

'Yeah. Sure. Give me half an hour.'

Elliot forces himself up and stands blearily. He needs air. Fresh air.

Padding across to the double doors that lead on to the ornate balcony, he pushes through into the world outside. The afternoon has slipped into evening, and he looks out across the fading emerald of the lawns. Laughter trips out from inside the marquee. Strands of stringed music filter the dusk. Another helicopter is landing. A slow pageant of limousines rolls slowly up the drive. The excitement pricks in him again. It's going to be a night to remember.

With this in his head he dances through into the ivory bathroom, turns on the taps, and empties a sachet of silken liquid into the steaming water. Silver bubbles rise up out of the sunken bath like miniature balloons.

He is in love with everyone, and everything. He's not great at parties, but this one feels different. He feels different. As if he's come through something, and now he's really on his way.

Dance on my heart.
Can't wait for this party to start

Evening Standard

ELLIOT HEATH AT HYDE PARK

PULL-OUT SPECIAL INSIDE

FOR MORE REVIEWS AND PICS SEE CENTRE PAGES

A NEW STAR RISING

ELLIOT HEATH AT HYDE PARK

By Lynne Bevan – Muse and Music

ELLIOT HEATH might be the Messiah of Music we've been waiting for.
Preaching his own brand of mood-moulding lyrics, Elliot was positively mesmerising in this afternoon's performance at Hyde Park.

Seemingly oblivious to the hellhot heat of the afternoon, Elliot played tunes from his recently released album, '*Trust Thing*', ending with the phenomenally successful '*Untouchable*', which sparked its way to the top of the charts earlier this year.

Emotionally bare, mysterious and hypnotic, there was something about the charge he put out that made the hairs stand up on the back of my neck. Even the most hard-baked of us reviewers were left shaking our heads in wonder.

If this boy keeps burning as bright as this, he'll be unstoppable as well as untouchable. Truly a gift from above!

Chapter Forty-Four

Amber stays in the shadows, sipping her cocktail and standing slightly back from the glow of the garden. Paper lanterns pour light down from the trees. Coloured bulbs blink out from bushes and shrubs.

A picture comes to her—a memory—a fairy grotto Dad took her to on one of his rare visits. 'Is there really such a thing as magic?' she'd whispered.

Her eyes narrow slightly now as she catches sight of Elliot, and she thinks if she couldn't manage to believe in it then, she might be able to manage it now. Elliot. Her Elliot. He's taken her breath away in that dinner jacket and tie. She's never seen him done up like that, and it churns her stomach just watching him. And it churns her up even more that he's talking to a bunch of girls—Heaven Scent. Laughing with them as if they're all having a good time, all in some superstar club together. She takes a bigger gulp of the cocktail. Heaven Scent are a smell from hell as far as Amber is concerned.

Her mind runs back to the fairy grotto again. They'd stopped by a well and she stared down into the crystal water at the glinting coins on the bottom. 'Do you think I can make a wish, Daddy?'

She's been doing a lot of that lately. Making wishes. Elliot's been hard to get hold of—impossible really. After they'd met up in the pub he started not answering his mobile—and then got the number changed. It drove her mad.

The 'wish making' with Dad went horribly wrong. 'It will come true, won't it?' she'd said, throwing her last coins into the water, its still surface shuddering, broken by slient ripples. His face tightened, and his grip on her fingers became bruising and hard. 'No. It's all crap.' She'd been young then—probably only about seven—but she knew crap wasn't a good word, especially in a fairy grotto.

'Ssssh, Daddy,' she said.

'Don't shush me.' His voice got louder. 'Like I said—it's all crap.' Other visitors stared, and then looked away quickly. Nice mums and dads with nice round-eyed children.

Amber had decided it was probably time to leave. 'I feel sick, Daddy,' she whispered. 'I want to go home.' And in a way it was true. She always ended up feeling sick and wanting to go home when she went out with Dad.

She smooths down the skirt of her green satin dress. It's short—even Declan boggled over it, the hypocrite. But who cares. And anyway, she's got good legs. Elliot has moved on from Heaven Scent now—thank God—but the bad thing is that he's talking to Traci Maran. Chatting. Just as if they're best friends. She doesn't want him talking like best friends with girls like Traci Maran. Once they're a proper item again she'll have her work cut out, keeping the Traci Marans away.

She didn't go out with Dad many more times after the fairy grotto day. He got a new girlfriend who had a daughter of her own, and there wasn't any room for Amber. She's lucky if she gets a Christmas card from him these days. Not that she cares. She's wiped him and the new girlfriend (who's probably an old hag by now)—and the poxy daughter (who's probably a young one)—from her mind.

Three new people have hooked up with Elliot. At least these ones are blokes. Blokes don't bother her. One of them is the lead singer from The Sessions, who have just arrived from Hyde Park. Helicoptered in, of course. The string quartet did a version of their last single 'Crazy Cookie', and everyone went mad dancing and singing. She wonders if Elliot hates all that—wonders if he thinks it should be 'Untouchable' they're all singing and dancing to. She bets he does. All of them must. They're all smiling and hugging and loveying now, but underneath they probably hate each other. How could they feel anything else?

It's maddening, not being able to go up to him, grab his arm and spin him away. But it's too soon. And anyway Declan's nearby, and she doesn't want Elliot to see them together. She's supposed to be back with him again. She had to do it—it was the only way she could get an invitation here—and once she'd read about the split from The Bitch in the paper, it was an easy game to play. They've been having a good time—or at least, that's what he thinks. But she'll never forgive him for putting The Bitch first, and he'll get a taste of what that feels like tonight.

She'd called Elliot at home when his mobile number became unattainable. His dad told her he'd moved up to London but wouldn't say where. 'Top Secret,' he muttered nervously, after he'd taken for ever to answer the phone. Well, she wasn't going to chase Elliot, and she definitely wasn't going to stand in the pathetic huddle of hopefuls that hung outside his dad's house, hoping he might make an Honorary Visit home.

It would have been good if he'd contacted her, but she knows he's just scared of getting dumped again. Tonight, once he sees her, he'll realize it's all going to be different. And in case he still needs to loosen up, she's got something in her handbag that will help both their wishes come true.

Chapter Forty-Five

'Drink, sir?' A waitress in a star-spangled dress glimmers in the twilight.

'Thanks.' Elliot takes one of the slender-stemmed glasses.

It's hard to pick out the celebrities from the staff here. Everyone is beautiful. Everyone is fantastic. The cocktail lightens his head, and he thinks he would like to eat. There's a table to his left, glistening with pastries and glazed meats and exotic fruits and salads, but every time he heads towards it somebody stops him.

'Hi, Elliot.'

'Hey.'

'Love the single.'

'When's the album coming out?'

His jaw aches from all the smiling.

There is dancing now. Girls laughing and kicking off their shoes. He can see Kris jiving with Sophie. They're good. He wishes he could learn to move like that, but he's never been great at dancing. Elliot's not sure how Kris managed to wangle Sophie an invitation, but it's good that she's there. It seems right that it's not just the front line stars who get to taste a night like this. And it's good to see Kris unwinding a bit.

'Drink, sir?'

'Cheers, mate.' He hadn't realized he'd knocked the last one back so fast. He needs to pace himself a bit better. There's already been champagne flowing during the speeches. He's not going to blow out tonight.

The tie is driving him nuts, and he wrenches it off suddenly, undoing his top button. One of the girls—a backing singer from Skunk Fudge—is already dancing in her bra and knickers, so he's got some loosening up to do. He spins the tie away, losing it in the bushes. His jacket is already gone, taken by one of the waiters.

The music softens. He moves back from the main throb of the action, leaning on a tree all twined with coloured lights. Couples meld into each other, girls' heads resting dreamily on blokes' shoulders.

He misses Anna. Even when he doesn't know he's thinking about her, he's thinking about her.

'Drink, sir?' He starts suddenly, surprised that the waitress has followed him into the shadows.

The girl stands in front of him, holding out a full glass. He squints at her. Blinks. Takes a moment to register the smiling girl with the clingy green dress and the fox-red hair.

'I need another drink. Fruit juice. Water. Something like that.' Elliot grins at the waiter and scans the tray.

'We've been dancing.' Amber hangs on Elliot's arm. 'Got a bit dried out.'

'Dried out. Danced out.' Elliot realizes he is giggling. The noise sounds strange, caught in the back of his throat. His jaw is working, chewing at nothing, and he wonders if the waiter has any gum. He pictures a choice of gums, all pricked with cocktail sticks and coloured paper umbrellas. The idea makes him want to giggle again.

'These on the left are grapefruit and lime.' The waiter's voice is slow. Running at the wrong speed. For some reason that seems funny too.

'We'll have two. No—four,' says Amber.

They chink them together as they knock them back. The waiter melts away. There is just a straggle of dancers left. 'The hard core,' Amber winds her arms round Elliot's neck. 'Come on.'

They shuffle in an easy circle. Elliot thinks he should keep an eye out for Kris, because he's disappeared. Probably had to get Sophie a car home. He's bound to be back. 'Keeping an eye out. That's weird, isn't it?' He pulls back from Amber slightly, studies her face. She looks fantastic, her fox hair whipped and wild.

'What?'

'That saying—"keep an eye out"—like taking a whole eye out and leaving it somewhere to watch for you, while you go off and do something else.'

She tips her head back, laughs, pulls him closer.

He laughs too. 'My feet hurt,' he says suddenly. He pictures a million pins, all stinging and burning. 'They're agony.'

'Take your shoes off then. I'll do it too. Heels are a nightmare on grass anyway.' Amber bends, slipping off her cream stilettos.

Elliot flops down on to the ground and undoes his laces. 'Let's chuck them.' Amber drops next to him. 'Together. One . . . two . . . three . . .'

He lifts his shoes at the same time she does, both of them whooping and shouting as four shoes go whirling up, tumbling through the air. 'Watch it!' a voice calls. 'You nearly hit me.'

'Ooops. Flying shoes. Lethal weapons,' whispers Amber.

'That's probably what foot soldiers use,' Elliot whispers back.

Amber laughs and leans against him again, then she pulls backwards. 'Come on. Get up. We have to keep dancing.'

'Have to keep dancing. Have to keep dancing,' Elliot shouts. The idea fizzes in him. He could dance for ever.

This dance is mad, wild and out of time. Elliot feels a surge of energy moving up through his bare feet, as if it's pushing through from under the ground. He pictures the grass, the tiny soft blades, the way each one uncurls and presses up beneath the hard soil. 'It's fantastic, isn't it?' he shouts.

'What is?'

'Grass. The way it grows.'

'Incredible.'

They are laughing again, and he thinks that he

hasn't laughed like this before, ever. He realizes, without letting it matter, that they have moved away from the other dancers, and are turning together into a shadowy corner, under some trees. Amber's arms are round him again.

The fairy lights blink a thousand colours. Elliot squints his eyes and the glow seems to stretch through the dark, painting the night. 'It's like somewhere magic, isn't it?' he says.

Amber stays quiet, her head on his shoulder. 'Do you think wishes ever come true?' she whispers at last.

Now it is Elliot who falls quiet, a race of scenes in his head. That audition. Signing the contract. All the way through to playing Hyde Park. 'Yeah.' He looks down at her. 'Sometimes.'

She puts her hand up to his face then. He can feel the heat of it, like a burn or a brand. As if the mark of her will stay on him for ever. He thinks maybe he should pull away, get back to what's left of the party. She's not Anna, she's not who he wants to be with. But they're only mates, and he feels good. So good. He just wants someone to hold on to. They stand together, swaying slightly, thin strands of party noise still weaving round them. Elliot thinks that there have never been this many stars filling the sky.

'Come on,' Amber says, and her voice is dreamy and gentle and part of this beautiful night. 'Let's go to your room.'

Dance all night.
This night feels new.
And it feels all right
to dance all night
with you.

Chapter Forty-Six

'He's mine.' The thought of this is delicious. Amber can almost taste it. Almost licks her lips.

She lies in the stark brightness of the room—they didn't get round to closing the curtains last night—and listens to him breathe. Shifting slightly and raising herself up on one elbow, she studies his face. Even asleep, he is beautiful.

It's taken a long time—longer than it's ever taken before—but it's been worth it. He's been worth it. And he'll keep being worth it. It startles her, to find herself thinking like this. She doesn't usually look ahead. She doesn't usually care enough. She gets a rush of need to put her arms around him, kiss him awake, but she stops herself. There will be plenty of that later. Right now, just in this moment, he is completely hers.

The room is fantastic, all of Eden carved on the ceiling. She smiles to herself. Very appropriate. Although things have moved on a bit since that apple. She wonders if he'll guess what really happened. But even if he suspects, he'll never know that it was her. There were so many people there. So many drinks left unattended. Anyone could have dusted some powder in—and there's no way she'd ever own up to it. It wasn't a bad thing to have done—it just helped him loosen up enough to relax with her. A harmless thing. No one could have been hurt by it. But he has to think that *he* chose to come on to *her*. Blokes need to think they've done the choosing.

He stirs slightly, his mouth moving as if he is locked in silent conversation. Then he groans and buries himself deeper into the quilt. She smiles. He is so lovely. So vulnerable.

She's not going to push her luck too far with him—at least, not at first. She's broken down his barriers, but he still has to chase her. Ring her. Wait for her. He might lose interest if she's too available. That's another of her rules. Never be too available. But if she plays it right, she can get him in such a state that he'll stuff the 'Untouchable' image. He'll breeze her name from a banner outside his stupid 'Top Secret' London apartment. And all those fans will be hating her. All those girls who have longed for him. She smiles again. To be the one who touches the Untouchable. Another delicious thought.

He wakes suddenly, jolting up as if from a bad dream, not even noticing her. She stretches her hand out, lazy as a cat, rubbing his arm with her knuckles.

'Hi.'

His head jerks round but his body pulls away, his face whitening. 'What happened?'

She pours him a smile, keeps her eyes honey warm. 'We did. We happened.'

She waits for him to find the memory. To smile back. But he doesn't. He shakes his head and his eyes are panicked. 'No.'

She shifts again, pushing the quilt away and sitting upright. Catching her reflection in the mirror opposite, she can see she's looking great. She runs her fingers lightly through her hair, letting it tumble down and round her shoulders. 'It's OK. It's what I wanted. What we both wanted.'

He shakes his head again. His hands are trembling and he looks like someone who's been punched. It hits her then that he might be having a really bad come-down. The Twitches. The Shivers. Paranoia. She's never had it that bad, but she's been with blokes who have.

She needs to be very gentle with him. 'Let's call down for hot tea. You look like you're feeling rough.'

It's as she stands to press the room service buzzer that it happens. His mobile. It's lying on the bedside table and tinning out the 'Untouchable' ringtone. 'That's the trouble with being famous.' She flicks a look back at him. 'You don't get any peace.'

She picks it up, goes to hand it to him, her eyes catching the caller's name running along the top of the screen. ANNA. She doesn't get it straight away. Isn't bothered. Anna could be a fat director. Somebody's boring secretary. A relative. 'Who's Anna?' she says playfully.

It's his voice that stalls her. Cracked and hoarse and full of fear. 'Don't answer it.'

'Why . . . ?'

'Please.'

They are both standing now, their eyes locked from opposite sides of the bed. The mobile feels hot in her hand. Ringing and ringing and ringing. Amber gets a picture of the invisible Anna, hearing the dial tone, thinking he must be still asleep. She thinks of a line running from her to Elliot. From Elliot to the Invisible Anna. From the Invisible Anna back to her. A triangle.

The ringing stops, but still neither of them moves. A second later the mobile bleeps—just once—again. A small symbol on the screen. The Invisible Anna has left a message.

'Aren't you going to listen to it?' A challenge creeps into Amber's voice that she doesn't quite understand. As if her instincts are running slightly ahead of what she knows.

'Not yet.' His eyes are hollowed out. Pained.

And then suddenly her knowledge catches up. She stays frozen for another moment, and then throws the mobile violently, hurling it against the mirror.

The glass cracks, a thin silver line running diagonally from top to bottom. 'You bastard,' she hisses, scrabbling on the floor for the crumpled green dress. Remembering she threw away her shoes. 'No one does this to me,' she spits round at him, heading for the door.

He is slumped on the edge of the bed, his back to her, his head in his hands. He doesn't look up as she goes.

HOT NEWS DAILY

TOUCHING THE UNTOUCHABLE

Elusive pop star Elliot plays more than his guitar after Hyde Park charity gig.

The lights changed for Westhill beauty Amber Palmer yesterday, as she revealed to us that there was more than champagne fizzing at the exclusive stars' celebration party last night.

'Untouchable . . . I don't think so,' giggled the curvy Miss Palmer, '. . . it was all pretty "hands on" really. We had a fantastic time.'

It's not the first time Amber and Elliot have made sweet music together either. 'We used to go out before he broke through,' she explained. 'But once the fame thing hit, his busy schedule forced us apart.'

Asked if last night might be the beginning of something more permanent, the luscious lovely's voice flattened out. 'Sadly, no. I love Elliot and I know he loves me, but I've had to turn away from him again. The world of pop means he's surrounded by so many girls, and he gets offers all the time. Everyone knows that blokes are weak in that department. It would be impossible to trust him, wouldn't it?'

Elliot Heath has built his whole act around his 'Hands Off' reputation. We bet a lot more hearts than Amber's will be broken now that the lock has been sprung, and we can all take a look at the sordid truth. Maybe he should change his slogan to 'Hands Everywhere' . . . ?

Paige Melder © Hot News Daily

Chapter Forty-Seven

Anna throws everything away. Postcards hurriedly scribbled from gig venues. A letter he wrote when he was down. The 'Hands Off' T-shirt and cap.

The phone starts up as she comes in from squashing it all into the bin, scrunching it down on top of the copy of *Hot News Daily*. Her heart seems cut with every ring. A physical pain. What if it's him?

'For you.' Mum's eyes are worried as she holds out the receiver. 'It's Lucy.'

Anna feels emptied out. Flattened. She hadn't realized how much she'd *wanted* it to be him, even though she'd probably have hung up if it had been. 'Hi.'

'Are you OK?'

'Trying to be.'

'You've seen it then?'

'Couldn't miss it.' It was on the stand outside the newsagent when she walked Boris up to the park before breakfast. Her hands shook as she bought it. Shook as she read it. She was sick when she got in.

'How you doing?'

'OK.'

'Are you staying home today?'

'Mum says I can—but I don't want to.' She wants

hub and hustle. Pupils shouting and pushing past her in corridors. The drone of voices teaching subjects she will struggle to listen to. She is suddenly afraid of silence.

Lucy's voice is determined. Taking charge. 'We're going out tonight, you and me. Dancing. To a club. I'll get you blotted and none of this will matter.'

Anna hesitates.

'Come on. Just go for it.'

'I . . . OK.'

'See you at school. I'm here for you. Be strong.'

She puts the receiver down, and goes back upstairs. Be strong. Be strong. She thinks of the words as hard metal. Big and bold, like guards at a gate. Protecting her. Stopping other thoughts from squeezing in through the railings. She gets ready for school. Does her hair. Puts on lipstick even though she knows she'll be told to wash it off. It strikes her suddenly that nobody except Mum and Lucy knew that she was even going out with him. And now she's yesterday's news, so who's even going to care?

She makes herself think that it isn't going to hurt for long. They hardly saw each other. The whole thing was just a game they were playing in their heads. She remembers her mantra. Put up with the life. A sort of trust thing. Could she really have put up with the life, long term? Always in the background. The Ghosted Girl. And did she really, really trust him?

The photograph in the paper showed a cheap,

tacky pose, but Anna could see that the girl was stunning. And if it wasn't her, there'd be others. Hundreds of them. Thousands. She's glad it's happened. Glad she's free of him.

Be strong. Be strong.

She pins back her hair. Splashes on her favourite vanilla perfume.

Be strong. Be strong.

It isn't until she turns to leave for school that she sees it.

Light and silver and magical, drifting above her bed. It had survived the whole concert, getting battered and bashed on the way out. Travelled with her on the train home. Floated round her bedroom. She'd thought of it as a sort of spirit watching over her until she saw him again.

This time the Be Strong guards can't hold the gates shut. Two names storm past them. Elliot Heath. Amber Palmer. Twining together through every spiked detail of that sleazy article. Suddenly she climbs on the bed, grabs the trailing string, pulls the balloon down and begins to punch it. Pummel it. It doesn't burst. It is stubborn. Alive. Her eyes blur as she grabs a pencil. Smacks it into the foil. Tearing at the middle of his name while her tears sting down. The life snaps out of it, the balloon suddenly crumpled.

She grips it in both hands, his name still visible, the letters scrunched and squashed. Then slowly she holds it to her face, burying herself in the cold silver. She isn't strong at all.

Unknown Host (Error 500)

The website you are trying to access has **not** been found.

This might be because:

- The site you are looking for has been deleted or moved.
- You have typed the Web address incorrectly.
  Please check, and try again.

Alternatively, please try to access a different website, such as http://www.abc.co.uk/ or http://www.abc.com/. If neither of these work, shut down and restart your computer, sign back on to ABC, and try visiting the website again.

For further assistance, go to the ABC Helpdesk: Internet Help.

Chapter Forty-Eight

'Sorry I didn't get here this morning.' Kris walks into Elliot's 'emergency' apartment with a pile of the day's papers. 'I managed to pick this lot up for you, though. There's loads today. You've obviously been busier than I thought.'

He watches Elliot sift through them all, bold headlines and busty beautiful girls.

MY HANDS-ON NIGHT WITH ELLIOT

SWEET SECRETS OF SEXY SUPERSTAR

A TOUCH OF 'THE UNTOUCHABLE'

'Busier than *I* thought too. I've never even seen this lot. Not one of them.'

Kris thinks he looks knackered. For a moment he gets a flashback of Elliot's dad, that first day he saw him. Maybe he shouldn't keep bringing these tabloids in, but Elliot had insisted. He'd been desperate to know what everyone was saying. Kris touches him on the shoulder, wishing he could say something positive. The truth is, he's feeling as gutted about this as Elliot—his own future's going down the drain too. But all they can do is sit it out. Although he's wishing he hadn't thrown so much money at the Elliot Project. From now on, he should work with two or three artists at one time. Keep more plates spinning. 'It'll all die down. Give it a couple more weeks.'

Elliot looks up from 'Sweet Secrets of Sexy Superstar' and shakes his head. 'It's been over three weeks already. Mud sticks.'

Kris takes the paper from him, and squints at the open page. It's a dingy, dark room even with the light on—he's told Elliot to keep the curtains drawn—so his eyes adjust slowly to the story about how Elliot signed 'Luscious Lavinia's' bra at the end of a gig one night—and that was only the beginning of what he got up to with the 'saucy sex siren'. He sits down on the lumpy, sagging sofa and folds the paper away. 'Well—at least it's publicity. It keeps you out there in front. They're not forgetting you.'

'They're not forgetting Amber Palmer either. There was a whole double page on her yesterday. Posing, of course. And she's been on breakfast TV.' Elliot slumps in the tired brown chair opposite, like somebody beaten.

Kris can't think what to say. He's seen all the publicity on Amber. There's even talk of her having her own teen chatshow—a crummy channel that nobody watches, but still, it could kick off a whole career for her. She's got herself in the public eye, and she'll do whatever she has to do to stay there.

He frowns down at the scraggy patterned rug that covers up most of the burn holes in the carpet. He'd have got the place painted and smartened up if he'd known he'd be putting Elliot in here, but it was a rush thing. Paparazzi outside Elliot's last apartment. Hate mail in the post. He couldn't risk leaving him there. He looks up slowly, only half aware of what he's thinking. 'Look—I know it feels rough but if Amber Palmer can make from it—then why don't we?'

'I don't get you.'

The ideas are only just coming, but the more they push through, the more they make sense. 'I reckon, with the right publicity, we can turn this around. Have you rising up phoenix-like from the ashes.'

'I still don't get you.'

Kris feels a new energy begin to surge through him. 'We build a new you. Shift your image.'

'What to—sex fiend?'

'Not exactly.' Kris is talking faster and faster. This could really work. He's sure of it. 'We find a way to play on that old innocence, and then have it that you've been woken up. We change the look. Sex up the sound—remember that experimental stuff you sometimes bring to rehearsals—well, it's things like that. A new, more dangerous, dirtier brand.'

Elliot's voice is empty. Flat. 'It's not just to do with that. There's people I've hurt. People I haven't . . .'

'I know.' Kris cuts across him. 'But if we swing this right, we can change all that. We might lose a few fans—but I reckon a lot of them will go with you. And there'll be new ones coming in too. Probably a bit older. And less fickle.'

'I don't want . . .'

Kris isn't going to listen to what Elliot wants. He is unstoppable now. 'Look—you haven't done anything *that* bad. It was just the surface image that got mud on it. So we let the public know you've grown out of that old skin, and you're moving on.'

'But you don't . . .'

Kris brushes him off with a wave of his hand. 'We can even set up a love affair for you. Find someone else—maybe someone sexy but older—who needs the publicity. Loads of stars do it. We won't let the story run for long, of course. There'll be a big public break up, and it'll bring in a whole new sympathy vote. Fans who know what it's like to get hurt. They'll really relate to the new brand. The new you.' He bends forward, gathering up the sprawl of papers that have slid to the floor, then squares a look at Elliot. 'Trust me. It's basic psychology. I'm going to get off and talk to a few people, but I'll be back. And it's going to be OK. By the time I'm finished, this whole Amber Palmer dirt will feel like it's stardust rained down on us from heaven.'

Chapter Forty-Nine

Elliot sits as Kris's footsteps grow fainter and fainter. From outside there is the bleep of an automatic key. An engine starts up, then slides away.

The whole weight of the apartment seems to press down on him. He gets up and walks to the bedroom. The kitchen. Back into the sitting room. The buzzing starts in his head again—it's been doing that a lot lately. He rubs at his ear, but the buzz doesn't go away. The place is chokingly hot, and stinks of must and old carpet. He wishes he could at least open the windows.

His thoughts wind their way round to Anna again. He was so close to telling Kris about her just now. So close to coming clean. Would it matter if he did? Would Kris really even care? What's she doing now?

He's sent her a thousand texts, but she never replies. He wonders what he'd be like if it was her story all over the papers. He wouldn't believe it. He'd try not to believe it. But maybe, just maybe, a worm of doubt would squirm its way in and burrow holes into all the good memories. Maybe he'd ignore her texts too.

He finds the remote and switches on the TV,

flicking through the channels. A quiz show. A hospital drama. An old bloke showing someone around his garden. Do people really watch stuff like this? Do people really want to watch chat shows hosted by Amber Palmer? It's all rubbish. The whole world's rubbish. But he leaves the gardening programme on. Afraid of the silence. Afraid of himself.

For the first time in his life, he can't hide inside his music. He tried that yesterday, and every note, every lyric, was like a brick in a wall. Heavy and hard, and no way of getting through. He told himself it was a trust thing. He told himself if he just stopped trying, it would come through on its own. But it didn't.

He reaches for his mobile. *Turn your phone on, Anna. Please. Please.* She's still switched off.

He could write to her, he's thought about that—but she might just scrunch the letter up. He'd never know if she'd stopped long enough to read it or not. And he wants her to hear him say sorry. He's still not sure how that night with Amber happened. When he runs his mind back through it, he can't get a grip on what he did, or why. That wired, buzzed, 'up for anything' madness just never feels like him. It was as if someone else had taken over. Some stranger in his head.

He glances at his watch. 4.15 p.m. She should be home from school by now. This time he punches in a new set of numbers—not her mobile, but the landline. He hasn't tried that yet—hasn't wanted to risk getting her mum—but maybe he should have done. Even if they hang up on him, at least Anna will know he's trying.

'Hello?'

He hesitates. It *is* her mum. 'This is Elliot. Can I speak to Anna?'

'Elliot?' Now it is her mum's turn to pause. 'I don't think she should talk to you.' She keeps her voice level and Elliot can't tell what she's thinking.

'Please. I just want to tell her . . .'

'I know, I know.' Anna's mum interrupts him gently. 'I'm sure it's a hard time, but Anna's really suffering. And she's got exams next week.'

'I won't keep her long.'

'She's upstairs revising at the moment. It's the first time she's even opened a textbook since—well, you know.'

'Please . . .'

'Elliot—there's nothing you can do or say. It's all too late.'

Too late. Too frigging late.

'If I could only . . .'

'Thank you for calling.' Anna's mum's voice changes suddenly. Bright. Crisp. Detached. 'But I really don't want any double glazing. Please don't ring again. Goodbye.'

The silence screams back at him. Anna must be near. She must have walked downstairs into the hall. The image—the vision—tears at him. The idea of her being by the phone and not knowing that he's on the other end. If he rings again now, she might get there before her mum. *Please. Please.* He presses the recall button.

Engaged.

Engaged.

He drops the mobile onto the chair. The old bloke on the TV is singing the glories of Michaelmas daisies. He remembers a daisy straggling up out of a stony grave. 'Life,' Anna had said that day. 'It's so wonderful. We mustn't pick it.' He blinks the TV off. Will all his life be made up of memories of her? Will she carry memories of him like that, or will she just get on with her wonderful life. Build an unpickable future without him?

He makes tea he doesn't drink. A sandwich that sticks in his throat. Slumps back in front of the turned off TV.

There is nothing you can do or say.

He thinks about all the stuff Kris said—about how he could pull it round. Grow him a new image. Even make up a love affair for him. How the hell is *that* going to look to Anna?

And then suddenly it hits him. He doesn't *have* to do it. He doesn't have to keep swinging like a tired puppet on the end of these strings.

Stuff the publicity.

Stuff the image.

He can find his way back to that failed audition bloke who sang sad songs in a Newton car park. He can find his way back to himself.

Kris will go bonkers. Obelisk will probably sue. He might never cut a disc again. But it'll all be worth it if it gets the message through to Anna about how gutted he is. And how sorry.

Standing up suddenly he goes over to the window, opening the curtains with a wrench. The late afternoon floods in, all the light and warmth on his hands, and his heart.

Stuff the paparazzi.

He's calling a taxi and he's getting away from here—he's going to Newton and he'll tell Anna what he's doing. She won't have to talk to him and she won't have to care, but at least she'll know he's doing it for her.

The most important thing is to let her know.

Against the sandbank of my mind
I feel the turning tide.

Chapter Fifty

Now that the taxi has got him here, Elliot doesn't know what to do. 'Can you hang on a minute,' he says. 'I've got to think something through.'

The driver glances into his rear-view mirror. 'This is a bus lay-by. I shouldn't really be parked here.'

'I won't be a sec. I just . . .' Elliot trails off. Just what? He's got to be prepared for her to scream at him. Throw stuff. Refuse to talk.

A bus pulls up behind them. The taxi radio crackles out indecipherable messages. The driver winds down his window and rests his arm on the frame. Whistling.

Elliot closes his eyes, takes a breath. Whatever she does, he'll deal with it. 'I'll pay by card,' he leans forward, handing it across.

As he signs the chit, the door to Anna's house opens, and she walks out. She is with the freckle-faced friend who was with her at the gig, and the friend is holding her arm, steering her along as if Anna has been reluctant to go.

Elliot is dazed. As if he's watching her in a dream. She looks fantastic in a yellow silk dress. Strappy high heels. Her hair floating long and loose, clipped back by something sparkling on one side.

He hands the chit back, and the driver folds it into his wallet. 'Cheers.'

'Cheers.' Elliot's heart is thundering. What will he say? How will he play it? It's always best not to think too hard. Let it come through on its own. A sort of trust thing. He moves towards the door as the driver comes round to let him out. Anna is passing, crossing the road only a metre away. Her head is tilted slightly as she listens to something the friend says. She is so close Elliot can see the diamond detail of the star in her hair. He thinks he can read the strain on her face. He has an odd sense of being sorry, and glad.

He wants to call out, but his throat is locked. He has to get this right.

She doesn't turn her head Elliot's way. She is still listening to her friend.

She doesn't see the van either, pulling out and swerving round the bus.

The screech of brakes comes too late. There is a smack of sound. Anna seems to twist backwards, her hands held out as if there is something she is trying to reach.

Chapter Fifty-One

Yakini Knight makes her way to the front of the hall, and stands at the edge of the stage. She's excited—not just because this assignment is a notch up from the ones her editor Brian usually sends her on—but also because she's got an interview booked backstage later.

She's going to be face to face actually talking to *the* Elliot Heath. And she's going to get the chance to write something decent for *Newton News* at last. She looks round the room. There aren't many here. Geoff Hobbs, who manages this place, told her earlier that there are loads of tickets left, which is sad. It would have made a brilliant story if he'd made a fantastic comeback, everyone besieging him the way they used to.

A slim, oriental-looking girl comes out on stage and checks the equipment. As well as two guitars and all the usual PA gear, there's a cello and a keyboard on opposite sides of the microphone. A man standing next to Yakini glances round at her, his eyes anxious. 'Poor turn out, isn't it?' He blinks rapidly as he speaks, plucking at the sleeve of his jacket.

'Maybe it'll fill up later.' She smiles back.

'Maybe it'll fill up later,' he mutters. He turns away again, nodding to himself, fixing his eyes on the stage.

Geoff Hobbs appears, holding out his hands to the straggled audience. They don't need quietening. Yakini jots down in her notebook that they are already subdued.

'. . . And now—' Geoff Hobbs is saying, '. . . he's been out of the scene for a while, but let's hear it for an old friend of The Edge—Elliot Heath.'

A ragged cheer goes up.

Elliot walks out into the spotlight.

Yakini jots down more details. He looks thinner than he used to in the 'Untouchable' days. But all of that image stuff is gone. He's just in baggy jeans and a T-shirt, his hair longer, slightly shaggy. You could pass him in the street—well, almost. You'd never *quite* pass a face like that in the street.

He stands for a minute, looking out at everyone. It's hard to tell what he's thinking, or feeling. Then he leans into his microphone. 'Thank you. For coming.'

There is a shake to his voice. A real pain in him. She can sense it. The audience senses it too because they press closer. Three girls to Yakini's left hold up a home-made banner. *Welcome Back*.

Two other girls lean into each other, the older one with her arm round the younger girl's shoulders.

'I dedicate this evening—every song—to my greatest friend ever. Anna Brook.'

The younger girl starts crying.

The clapping only fades as Elliot hits the first chord. It's a song Yakini has never heard him do. 'The First Time'.

Yakini notes down that the image might have changed, but not the voice. Or the quality of the sound. Her own skin prickles and her eyes well up. She remembers a scratching of detail about Anna Brook. She was a local girl, and she was involved in an accident around the time all the 'Kiss and Tell' rubbish was going on. Her death got a bit of publicity because Elliot had happened to be on the scene for some reason, but the hype about his split from Kris Kowper soon overshadowed the Anna Brook story.

She hadn't realized Elliot had known Anna Brook so well.

As 'The First Time' ends, the audience clap and call again.

'Elliot!'

'Still love you, Elliot.'

'Good to see you back.'

He stands quietly, his head slightly bowed. Yakini notices an older couple come in. The woman nods across and smiles at the muttering man, and then stands with her partner on the opposite side of the room.

Elliot looks up, his voice quiet but level. 'Thank you. This one's a bit more up-beat. It's called "Velvet and Wild Roses".'

Another cheer. More clapping. Yakini gets the feeling Elliot could sing to an iceberg, and it would melt against the sound.

She wonders if she could use that in the article—a theme around melting lyrics. She knows Brian likes things told straight, but maybe she could turn him round a bit if she writes well. She needs to prove to him that just because she doesn't have a degree, it doesn't mean she has to stay stuck on small stories for ever.

She wants to be big one day—a music journalist. And she wants to write articles that are beautiful, to develop a voice so that even if she doesn't put her name to the writing, everyone will still know it is her. Journalism isn't always trashy and manipulative. She wants to make hers a sort of art.

'Thank you—thank you. Another dance number for you. This is "Taking the Grey Away".'

Most of the audience are dancing. Waving. Many seem to know the words. The spotlight on Elliot dims. A cellist and a keyboard player join him on the stage and he moves into a strange, haunting song about a turning tide.

Yakini wonders if Elliot's dad is here. He apparently sold his house to help Elliot out when everything went wrong. He had to buy himself free from his record label, and it cost him most of what he'd earned from his Untouchable days.

Kris Kowper didn't take a cut though. Yakini read somewhere that he was broken up about the whole thing, but he was back with a new project now. Some girl band he'd formed after an audition.

The next run of songs drifts by in a blur.

'Cappuccino Lady'. 'Pictures on My Heart'. 'Long Long Time Without You'. The sounds are amazing. Experimental. Cutting edge. But they all have that depth running through them. Something sweet and yearning and always just out of reach.

A lot of the audience have their arms round each other now, a weave of bodies embracing round the room. Yakini thinks she has never seen anything like it. Not at a small venue like this. So much warmth. So much love. She finds herself lost in the roll of it, and hadn't realized they were so close to the end of the evening. And she's sorry it's nearly finished. She could have stood here and listened for ever. She gets a sense then of the world turning. Rubbish things happen—she's had her share of that—but music like this lifts you. It gives you the belief that there's something more.

'Thank you. You've been a great audience. I hope you've enjoyed tonight. Your support means a lot—probably everything.' Elliot pauses. Swallows. That shake in his voice again. 'I've come to the last number now. Thank you once again for listening. And thanks too to anyone who has sent e-mails and letters of support over the last year. And my final thank you is, as it always will be, to Anna. This song is called "Wreathe You With Daisies".'

As the song washes round the hall, Yakini dodges under the arms of the audience, most of them now holding lighters or mobile phones, the glow magical and beautiful. She edges her way to the dressing room.

'Yakini Knight,' she says to the bouncer on the door. 'I've got an interview booked.' She has to say it twice because he is watching the stage, and when she finally catches his attention he blinks and rubs damp eyes with the back of his hand. It's amazing, a muscle hard bloke like him. She shows him the stamped identity card that will back up where she's from. Elliot's new foreign sounding manager—May Ling or something—seemed anxious about security when Yakini rang, and she couldn't blame her. He'd had a really rough ride with the press. But Elliot and his team needn't worry about her. She's on his side. Anything she writes will let the world know—well, *Newton News* readers at least—that she thinks he's awesome. It's a start. A new beginning for him.

The bouncer lets her through and she stands in the dressing room, checks her face in a cracked wall mirror, and waits.

Stumble through the daisies.
Wreathe you songs of love.
Hope you stroke
their petals
from above.